"REPEAT MY ORDER, MR. HUNTER!"

"Sir," said Hunter in a bare whisper, "I can't."

"You are relieved of your position!" snapped Ramsey. "COB, remove him from control. And get Lieutenant Zimmer in here, now!"

The COB took a tentative step forward. Hunter stubbornly held his ground.

"Captain, under operating procedures governing the release of nuclear weapons, we can only launch our missles if both you and I agree. This is not a formality, sir. This is expressly why your command must be repeated! It requires my assent. And I do not give it!"

"You son of a bitch!" cursed Ramsey. "Chief of the boat, as captain and commanding officer of the USS *Alabama*, I order you to place XO Hunter under arrest on the charge of mutiny!"

CRIMSON TIDE

a novel by

RICHARD P. HENRICK

Based on the screenplay by
MICHAEL SCHIFFER
from a story by
RICHARD P. HENRICK and **MICHAEL SCHIFFER**

AVON BOOKS ◆ NEW YORK

CRIMSON TIDE is an original publication of Avon Books. This work has never before appeared in book form. This work is a novel based on a screenplay by Michael Schiffer and a story by Richard P. Henrick and Michael Schiffer. Any similarity to actual persons or events is purely coincidental.

AVON BOOKS
A division of
The Hearst Corporation
1350 Avenue of the Americas
New York, New York 10019

Copyright © 1995 by The Walt Disney Company
Submarine schematic diagram and SUBASE, Bangor information courtesy of the U.S. Navy
Published by arrangement with The Walt Disney Company
Library of Congress Catalog Card Number: 95-90089
ISBN: 0-380-78323-1

First Avon Books Printing: June 1995

AVON TRADEMARK REG. U.S. PAT. OFF. AND IN OTHER COUNTRIES, MARCA REGISTRADA, HECHO EN U.S.A.

Printed in the U.S.A.

RA   10   9   8   7   6   5   4   3   2   1

ACKNOWLEDGMENTS

Having been involved with *Crimson Tide* since its inception, I'm indebted to a number of individuals who made my participation in this project possible. First off, a special thanks to Michael Lynton, Ricardo Mestres, and Mike Stenson of Hollywood Pictures, who gave me my initial "sailing orders." Senator James Exon of Nebraska and Bruce Blair of the Brookings Institute helped guide me through the intricacies of the command and control of nuclear weapons aboard Trident. My sincere appreciation also goes out to Hunter Heller of the Walt Disney Company, and the moviemakers—Jerry Bruckheimer, Don Simpson, Lucas Foster, Mike Moder, and Tony Scott. And last, but definitely not least, special thanks to Michael Schiffer and Quentin Tarantino, the master screenwriters, who made our story come alive. Michael, as far as I'm concerned, you'll always be the Skipper!

"Canst thou draw out Leviathan . . . ? None is so fierce that dare stir him up . . . I will not keep silence concerning his mighty strength, or his goodly frame . . . Who can penetrate his double coat of mail? . . . Out of his belly go flaming missiles; sparks of fire leap forth . . . And as he raises himself up from the sea, even the mighty are afraid; for though Trident's sword reaches him, it does not avail."

—Job 41:1–26

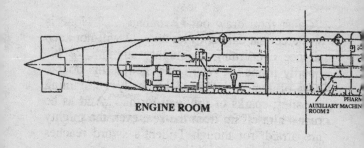

ENGINE ROOM

AUXILIARY MACHINE
ROOM 2

PHARM...

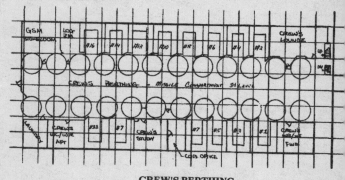

CREW'S BERTHING

SCHEMATIC DRAWINGS FOR AN
OHIO-CLASS SUBMARINE

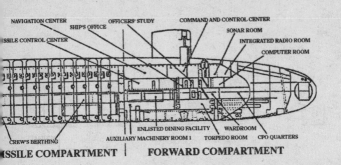

NAVIGATION CENTER
SHIP'S OFFICE
OFFICERS' STUDY
COMMAND AND CONTROL CENTER
SONAR ROOM
INTEGRATED RADIO ROOM
COMPUTER ROOM
MISSILE CONTROL CENTER

ENLISTED DINING FACILITY
WARDROOM
CREW'S BERTHING
AUXILIARY MACHINERY ROOM 1
TORPEDO ROOM
CPO QUARTERS

MISSILE COMPARTMENT | **FORWARD COMPARTMENT**

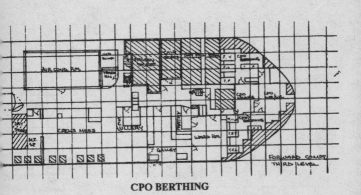

AIR COND. RM.

CREWS MESS

SCULLERY

WARD RM.

GALLEY

FORWARD COMPT.
THIRD LEVEL

CPO BERTHING

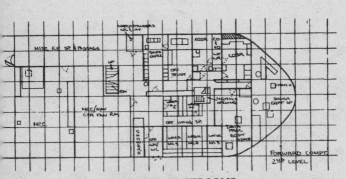

MISC EE SP. & PASSAGE

SHIP'S OFFICE

OFF. STUDY

MCC/NAV
CTR FAN RM.

MCC

OFF.
WAY
WC

FORWARD COMPT.
2ND LEVEL

OFFICERS' STATEROOMS

It was a muted growling sound that caused Vladimir Radchenko to cut short his stride in midstep. The solidly built, fifty-nine-year-old politician silently planted his booted right heel firmly on the narrow earthen path and intently scanned the surrounding forest. A thick wood of mature birch trees met his glance, their textured white trunks collectively bending in the gathering breeze like a bobbing fleet of sailing ships on a brownish green sea.

The air temperature had noticeably dropped since he began his hike, and Radchenko pulled up the fur-trimmed collar of his greatcoat to counter the chill. The first snows of autumn had already fallen, hinting at the harsh Russian winter that would soon follow. A native Siberian by birth, Radchenko was certainly no stranger to this change in climate, and in many ways, the arrival of winter invigorated him.

Beyond the softly creaking tree limbs and the distant, harsh cry of a lonely raven, rose the alien growl that had initially caught his attention. It seemed to come from somewhere ahead, and he cautiously continued down the footpath to identify its source.

The twisting trail of soft earth led him up a slope to the top of a small rise. There he briefly halted to regather his breath. Trying his best to ignore a desperate craving for a cigarette, he instinctively took cover behind a fallen cedar trunk, when the familiar growl once more sounded, this time more clearly.

With the practiced ease of a skilled hunter, his glance swept the wood beyond the rise. A cascading brook cut the footpath there, its bubbling gurgle calling to him like a long-lost friend. It was while coming to the realization that he had been spending too much time in a deadened city environment lately, that he spotted a slight movement on the stream's far bank. There, less than a quarter of a kilometer distant, was a magnificent, fully grown grey wolf. The creature was in the process of devouring a freshly killed fawn, whose bloody carcass was split open at the abdomen.

Ever the watchful carnivore, the wolf would tear off a mouthful of meat, chew it thoroughly, swallow it, then carefully survey the area before taking another bite. It was while it was in the process of scanning the forest that another growl escaped its lips. Part-warning, part-contentment, this primal sound overrode the ever-gathering wind and caused shivers of excitement to course up Radchenko's spine.

To encounter such an elusive creature this close to Moscow was an incredible stroke of good fortune on his part! Finding it hard to believe that the Kremlin was less than forty kilometers due south, he did his best to hide his bulky torso behind the fallen trunk so he could continue to watch the wolf without scaring it away. He had little fear of the wolf.

While wandering the taiga as a youth, he had seen his fair share of wolves. Though most of his childhood friends reacted to those encounters with dread, Radchenko had always had a great respect for the wolf. It was an intelligent predator, at the very top of its food chain. Only man, or a brave bear, threatened it. From his schoolbooks he had learned that the wolf had a close family unit, one that often hunted as a collective entity, showing no mercy to its prey.

It was this latter quality that excited Vladimir's imagination and caused him to closely relate to the wolf. As far as he was concerned, there could be no more noble creature in all the forest. Not hampered by such human frailties as morality or ethics, the wolf lived to procreate and feed, oblivious to any so-called higher being or alternative plane of existence. Surely it lived in a clean, orderly world where might was right and only the strong survived to pass on their genes to the next generation.

How unlike this was to mankind's current state. Having long ago lost the primal spark that once connected the human race to the primal earth sphere, man had evolved into a pathetic, weak-willed species of followers, blinded by petty consumerism, and stripped of spirit by the need for instant gratification. Having long ago lost the ability to stalk prey and patiently initiate a successful hunt, modern man would do well to study the wolf and rediscover those all-important virtues.

...igorated by his thoughts, Radchenko was abruptly called back to the present when the wolf suddenly dropped the mouthful of meat that it was chewing and peered up into the heavens. The Siberian followed the direction of the creature's glance, and his gaze focused on a small patch of dark grey sky, barely visible through the swaying birch limbs.

It was as the first snow flurries fell against his leathery cheeks that he heard a distant, deep, clattering racket. It was evident that his friend the wolf had also heard this ever-increasing noise, for it suddenly abandoned its meal and went scurrying away into the woods beyond. Sorry to see it go, Radchenko redirected his steely-eyed glance upward and soon enough viewed the object responsible for scaring away the wolf.

Looking every bit the lethal, flying predator that it was, the distinctive dark green body of a Mil Mi-8 helicopter roared overhead. Its squat, elongated fuselage sported seven prominent portholes, with a red, five-pointed star visible beside the aft window.

Suddenly aware of the time, Radchenko stood and anxiously looked at his watch. He found himself genuinely surprised at the late hour and, after silently chastising himself, turned around and began quickly walking down that portion of the trail leading back to his dacha.

It took him the better part of a quarter of an hour to complete this hike. By the time he reached the clearing where his country home was located, a thin coat of perspiration matted his wrinkled forehead. The flurries were falling more steadily now, and a welcoming column of thick black smoke rose from the cottage's chimney.

As he passed by a cord of firewood that he had recently chopped himself, he spotted the Mil helicopter parked on the far side of the dacha. Two soldiers could be seen milling beside the aircraft, smoking cigarettes. Ever craving a smoke himself, Radchenko walked up to the cottage's front door, wiped the snow off his boots, and then entered without knocking.

The alien warmth inside was at first stifling. He quickly stripped off his coat, hat, and gloves, and proceeded into the adjoining living room, called there by the sound of voices.

Gathered there, beside the blazing fireplace, was a trio of familiar individuals. His wife Anna had apparently just come in from the kitchen, along with a silver serving cart displaying a selection of food and drink.

It was obvious that no one was aware of Vladimir's presence, and he took a moment to size up the two men, standing beside his wife, who were busy filling their plates with appetizers. Physically dominating this duo was the tall, erect figure of Viktor Sorokin. The white-haired former defense minister was dressed in a well-tailored, grey pinstriped suit, and even while dishing out a hearty serving of red caviar, appeared to be the picture of dignified suaveness.

Sorokin's curly-haired associate was in every way his physical opposite. Boris Arbatov carried his five-foot, five-inch frame with a perpetual stoop. The veteran political analyst was attired in one of his infamous baggy brown suits, whose trouser cuffs extended well over his scuffed leather shoes, and did little to compliment his portly figure. With his stubby hands busy adjusting the fit of his bent wire rim glasses, and piling his piece of rye bread with as much herring, onion, and sour cream as possible, Arbatov was caught by complete surprise when the newcomer in their midst loudly cleared his throat.

"Good afternoon, Comrades," greeted Radchenko lightly. "Looks like I got here just in time to pour the vodka."

Anna looked up from her duties and warmly smiled. "My, just look what the wind blew in. I'm glad that you decided to join us, husband."

Vladimir stepped forward and hugged his wife, while kissing her on each cheek. "Thanks for taking care of my guests," he said with a wink.

Both Viktor Sorokin and Boris Arbatov put down their plates to accept a hug from their host, who added, "I apologize for my tardiness, Comrades. While taking my customary after-lunch stroll, I sighted a large grey wolf feeding on a deer carcass. I'm afraid viewing this magnificent creature momentarily diverted me from my immediate responsibilities, and I all but forgot the time until your helicopter flew over."

"A wolf, you say, Vladimir Ilyich?" reflected Sorokin. "It's indeed unusual to spot such a creature this close to the city limits."

"During the Great Patriotic War, wolves by the hundreds were found wandering right down Red Square," intervened Boris Arbatov as he turned his attention back to his herring. "The old babushkas used to try to shoot the beasts for a welcome addition to their near empty stewpots.''

Radchenko responded while reaching out for the crystal decanter that graced the cart's bottom shelf. ''I can't help but wonder whose efforts were the most successful, the wolves' or our babushkas'? From the fierce looks of the creature I just left in the birch forest, I certainly wouldn't want to have to tangle with such a beast.''

He proceeded to uncork the decanter and fill three tiny stemmed glasses with a super-cooled clear liquid.

''Can I pour you a drink, Anna?'' he politely asked.

Anna's blue eyes sparkled as she shook her head that she wasn't interested. ''I'll pass, husband. Right now I'd better return to the kitchen and attend to the bread that I'm baking. Just shout if you need anything else.''

As she left the room, Radchenko handed each of his guests a goblet. He then raised his own glass and toasted.

''To the glory of our beloved Motherland!''

Boris Arbatov was the first to drain his glass and he appreciatively smacked his lips. ''This vodka is very tasty, Vladimir.''

''I'm glad that you like it,'' returned Radchenko, after swallowing a mouthful of the fiery spirits. ''It's distilled from potatoes grown in my hometown, on the shores of Lake Baikal.''

Radchenko went on to fill a plate with a selection of breads, caviar, and herring, which he placed on a small table beside the fireplace. After refilling their glasses, he beckoned his guests to have a seat on the sofa. As they did so, he added another log to the fire. It snapped and hissed its gratitude.

"Anna was just telling us that you spent much of the morning splitting firewood," said the former defense minister, his gaze locked on the dancing flames. "Be careful, Vladimir Ilyich. We wouldn't want to lose you to a heart attack."

"Nonsense," Vladimir retorted. "Since I gave up smoking, I never felt so good. This old ticker of mine is in fine shape, and the wood chopping helps me forget how much I really miss my cigarettes."

Boris Arbatov was all set to light a cigarette of his own, when he remembered his manners. As one might pull back a word from the tip of one's tongue, he did his discreet best to stow away his cigarette pack without Radchenko's noticing, and the portly political advisor redirected his attention to his food.

Radchenko readdressed his guests after sampling some caviar. "How was the flight from Moscow?"

"You know how much I enjoy traveling by helicopter, Comrade," said Sorokin sarcastically. "I'm ever thankful that your dacha's only a few minutes away from the city's center."

Arbatov was quick to add, "Although I'm not much of a flyer myself, having the services of that helicopter sure beats having to rely on an automobile."

Radchenko grunted, and decided that it was time to get down to business. "I gather that you brought along the photographs that you spoke of this morning?"

Viktor alertly reached for the black calfskin

briefcase that stood beside the sofa. He snapped it open, removed a large manila envelope, and from that extracted a stack of black-and-white photographs. The former defense minister pointed to the top photo. It showed an aerial view of a heavily wooded hillside, whose surface was scarred by dozens of jagged bomb craters.

"This first bomb damage assessment shot comes to us from the sensor pod of a Tupolev Tu-20 reconnaissance aircraft. The location is a hillside north of Tuzla, in Bosnia Herzegovina. Our overflight took place this morning, shortly after daybreak."

Radchenko thoughtfully examined this photograph, as well as the next aerial shot, which displayed a close-up of one of the craters. The remains of an overturned artillery piece could just be made out, as well as several twisted human corpses draped beneath the gun's undercarriage.

"The bombs took out an entire Serbian artillery regiment," continued Viktor. "They were delivered with frightening accuracy, and it's feared that over one hundred Serbian soldiers lost their lives during the attack."

A look of stunned disbelief filled Radchenko's flushed face, and he sorted through several more photos showing similar carnage. His hands began to shake slightly upon coming across a photograph of an airborne jet fighter. The sleek, grey fuselage of the airplane had no identifiable markings, yet its pilot was caught in the act of flashing the photographer that universal sign of contempt known as "the finger."

Quick to note Radchenko's reaction to this snapshot, Viktor continued his commentary with rising emotion. "This F/A-18 Hornet was photographed by the Tu-20, directly over the target area. It appears to have been caught in the midst of a bomb damage assessment survey of its own. Our crew was able to follow it all the way to the Adriatic Sea, where it subsequently landed on the deck of its mother ship, the American Nimitz-class carrier *George Washington*."

As Radchenko examined the final photo in the series, which showed an aerial shot of the F-18 landing on the deck of the immense carrier, his voice quivered with restrained anger. "Is this the floating airbase from which the strike on the Serbian positions originated?"

Viktor somberly nodded that it was, and Radchenko's rage erupted. "Do you realize what this means, Comrades? By directly attacking our Serbian brothers, the Americans have committed an act of war against the Russian people!"

Radchencko's face turned a brilliant beet red, and there could be no hiding his anger as he shakily sorted through the stack of photographs one more time.

"Less than an hour ago, the U.S. president acknowledged America's involvement in the air strike," revealed Boris. "In a brief statement to the American people, he admitted ordering the attack in response to what he called a flagrant act of aggression against the people of Tuzla by rogue elements of the Serbian Army, in direct violation of the U.N.–brokered peace treaty."

"And the nature of this so-called flagrant violation?" asked Radchenko.

This time it was Viktor who answered. "We believe it occurred when one of the Serbian artillery pieces accidentally misfired. The U.N. observers in Tuzla mistook this shell for a full-scale attack, and it was under their auspices that the air strike was called in."

"I'm almost afraid to ask how our own brave president reacted to America's admission of guilt?" spit Radchenko with disgust.

"Our fearless leader refused to comment on the incident, until a full-scale U.N. investigation is completed," Boris said. In years past, had he dared say these words, he would have said them only to his sweating palms. But not now, although still the urge was there.

A tone of utter disbelief flavored Radchenko's emotional response. "A valued ally is attacked without provocation, and our president dares to wait for a U.N. investigation before issuing a response? My heavens, he's a bigger fool than we ever suspected! His inaction once more demonstrates to the entire world how Russia has become nothing more than a third-rate nation, a lackey of the Western Capitalist powers. Has he already forgotten the meaning of pride, and the value of a commitment to an ally? Surely this is Mother Russia's lowest hour, with each one of us responsible for the shame that now stains us."

As if reacting to this outburst, the fire crackled loudly. Boris Arbatov removed a handkerchief from his pocket and patted dry the sweat that stained his upper lip, before expressing himself.

"Both Viktor and I share your anger, Vladimir. Our president's inaction is inexcusable, and we feel that now is the best time to appeal to the people and initiate the great revolution that we have long dreamed of.''

Viktor Sorokin looked at his watch and added. ''In less than two hours, the Parliament is scheduled to reconvene. We have arranged to have you open the session, Vladimir Ilyich.''

''And what better way to do so, than with a statement voicing your outrage?'' continued Boris. ''The people are open to our message like never before. With the government's disastrous policy in Chechnya still fresh in their minds, we believe that this dastardly American bombing is the primer that will spark a firestorm of united protest by the Russian people!''

Vladimir Radchenko thoughtfully pressed at his wide temples, then looked each of his anxious guests full in the eyes before cracking the barest of sardonic grins. ''So the hour of truth is finally upon us, Comrades,'' he said in a whisper. ''I accept your challenge. I, too, feel it deep in my heart, that the time is right. For the third time this century, the cry of revolution will fill the air. We mustn't deceive ourselves into thinking that this transfer of power will go smoothly. Our pathetic alcoholic president will surely not go down without a fight.''

''As previously discussed, the movement is well prepared to respond to his anticipated reaction,'' Boris said.

From his briefcase Viktor pulled a thick file folder with a bright red hammer and sickle engraved on its cover. ''Inside this dossier,'' he said, ''is the manner in which we intend to respond to his anticipated suspension of the Parliament and declaration of martial law.''

Knowing full well the contents of this dossier, Radchenko accepted the folder and slyly grinned. ''Something tells me that the first active elements of our revolution have already begun.''

Viktor nodded. ''They have, Comrade. Anticipating your reaction to the American air strike, I took the liberty of informing General Chernavin to ready his troops. They will be prepared to move out en masse from Vladivostok by the time we arrive in Moscow this afternoon. As far as the authorities in Art'om are concerned, Chernavin's division is in the area for a realistic training exercise that's to take place on the perimeter of the missile launch compound.''

''And our submarines?'' asked Radchenko.

''The Akulas are fueled and ready to set sail on your orders,'' Viktor answered.

A look of excitement crossed Vladimir Radchenko's handsome face as he peered into the fire. The blazing embers hissed loudly, and he found his thoughts momentarily transferred back into the woods outside the dacha. Surely the wolf had devoured the deer carcass completely by now. Its actions were directed by a primal will that recognized no right or wrong. The wolf's example would point the way for Radchenko's own behavior in the difficult days that would surely follow. Ever hopeful that he'd be able to tap the level of ferocity needed for the successful predator to endure, he reached out for the crystal decanter and refilled his guests' glasses.

''To the rebirth of our Motherland!'' he toasted,

after filling his own glass with the fiery potato vodka. "May the spirit of the hunter fill our hearts with fortitude and provide us strength for the revolution that will soon engulf our homeland!"

2

A world away from the political intrigues of Vladimir Radchenko and his cronies, another toast had just been offered, not to glorify revolution, but instead to celebrate the miracle of birth. This afternoon's birthday party was being held at the Silverdale, Washington, home of Lieutenant Commander Ron Hunter and his wife, Julia. The Hunter family was new to the Pacific Northwest, having recently arrived from Norfolk, Virginia. Like U.S. Navy families everywhere, they were used to such moves, which usually occurred like clockwork every two years.

The Navy community was well aware how difficult such transitions could be for a family, thus extra care was taken to create a warm, stable home environment, especially for the children. Having just turned a precocious five years old, Robin Hunter was totally unaware of how her parents had shepherded her across the entire continent and into a new home, with the least amount of noticeable inconvenience. As far as Robin was concerned, the only differences between their last address in Virginia and their new home were the thick poplar forest that currently surrounded their house and the frequent rains that fell.

Though Robin missed her old friends, the new neighborhood offered her an entirely new cast of boys and girls to play with. Because they were of similar age, and their parents were for the most part active members of the U.S. Navy, her new playmates shared much in common. Thus this afternoon's party was a success.

Robin's father was particularly delighted to see how much his daughter was enjoying herself. Throughout the move, his worst fear had been that she wouldn't be able to adjust to her new environment. How groundless his worries were turning out to be! Much like her mother, Robin was demonstrating a remarkable ability to make new friends quickly. She'd only just met many of the children attending her party, yet already they were acting like old playmates.

Per the strict instructions of his wife, he was doing his best to capture as much of the fun as possible on videotape. The children were presently gathered inside the living room, where "Bob the Magician" was entertaining them. Julia had learned about Bob from a neighbor, and though Ron had initially balked at the idea of hiring him, he eventually relented. Happy now that he had done so, he made certain to capture on tape the look of delight that filled his daughter's face as the magician began a pyrotechnics display that ended with his conjuring a live dove out of thin air.

Beneath gaily colored helium balloons that covered the ceiling, the children and a small group of supervising adults applauded enthusiastically. Lieutenant Peter Ince, a longtime friend who had moved out from Norfolk six months earlier, whispered to Hunter, "If you ask me, that trick alone was worth the forty-five bucks that you had to shell out to hire the guy."

Without pulling his eye from the camcorder's lens, Hunter replied. "What do you mean, forty-five bucks? That guy cost me a hundred and a quarter, and that's without the tip!"

Oblivious to this exchange, the tuxedo-clad magician stowed the dove away in a cage and addressed his rapt audience. "Now I need a volunteer, and a brave one at that."

Almost instantaneously the hand of every child shot up into the air. Hunter noted that his daughter was particularly anxious to be selected, and he couldn't help but grin as the magician once more addressed his audience.

"I'd prefer it if this particular volunteer was someone who was born on October 17, 1991."

Most of the children seemed to be unsure of their exact birthdates, including Robin. She looked up to her mother for reassurance, then, told that this birthdate was her own, immediately stood up and proudly made her way to center stage. Unfortunately, Hunter's camera battery picked this inopportune moment to give up the ghost. He excused himself to make his way into the kitchen, where a spare battery hopefully awaited him.

Much to his relief, he found the spare on the kitchen countertop, inside the charger. The birthday cake was sitting beside it, and he couldn't resist dipping his finger into the cherry icing and pulling a tiny drop away from the base. As he brought it to his lips, his glance was drawn to the nearby television set. Someone had left it turned on, and dozens of fast-moving tanks filled its small screen. The image of a newscaster filled the bottom portion of the screen, and Hunter turned up the volume to listen to his report.

"It was at 10:00 A.M. Moscow time that the Russian Parliament was suspended and martial law declared. Shortly afterward, the first tanks began arriving in Red Square. With the government in crisis, the Russian Republic began entering what can only be described as a state of civil war.

"This crisis quickly escalated when yesterday, at dawn, Vladimir Radchenko and his rebel army forces seized control of a military installation outside the Russian city of Vladivostok. As loyalist army units moved in to encircle Radchenko, it was learned that the military base that the rebels had managed to seize included an unknown number of intercontinental ballistic missiles outfitted with an unspecified number of nuclear warheads. And it was only an hour ago that Radchenko threatened to use these missiles on the United States and Japan should anyone, including the Russian Army, attempt to move in on him."

"Sweet Jesus!" muttered Hunter, his daughter's birthday party all but forgotten.

As the television screen filled with a picture of the rebel leader perched on top of a tank, Peter Ince arrived in the kitchen. His shipmate's voice seemed to be coming from an altogether different plane of existence.

"I don't think that you want to miss this next trick, Ron. Bob the Magician is about to levitate your daughter between two folding chairs.''

Hunter's failure to respond caused Ince to join him in front of the television set. As the scene shifted to an exterior shot of the Pentagon, they listened to the newscaster continue.

''Based on Radchenko's history, his threat to launch nuclear missiles can't be viewed as an idle one. Thus, at this very moment, Congress is meeting in emergency session, while the president is sequestered with the Joint Chiefs of Staff.''

''Radchenko's threatened to launch nuclear missiles?'' interjected Ince. ''How in the hell did he get the release codes?''

Hunter responded while reaching out to turn down the television's volume. ''What I don't understand is why the phone's not ringing.''

''Maybe it's not as bad as it looks,'' Ince offered.

Though Hunter knew better, he nevertheless concurred. ''Maybe you're right.''

No sooner were these words spoken than Ince's beeper activated. A fraction of a second later the kitchen phone began ringing. Without having to answer it, Hunter knew in an instant just who the caller was.

Exactly one hour later, a white van pulled up to the Hunter residence. It arrived in the midst of a torrential rainstorm. The van's khaki-clad driver leaped from the vehicle with a golf umbrella in hand and sprinted up the brick walkway to the covered front porch.

As the driver hurriedly rang the front doorbell, he heard singing inside, so he loudly rapped on the door four times with its brass knocker.

When the door finally opened, it revealed a tall, slender, African-American naval officer dressed in the khaki uniform of a lieutenant commander. The driver noted the golden dolphins that graced the officer's chest, and as he looked up to address him, he sensed a certain polite gentleness to this officer's demeanor.

"Lieutenant Commander Hunter?" he asked.

"I'll be right with you, Chief," said the submariner, as he turned to address the slim, attractive woman who stood close behind him.

"Honey," he said to her softly, "as soon as I know something, I promise I'll call."

As they kissed and hugged each other, the driver caught a glimpse of what appeared to be a children's birthday party taking place inside. Barely aware of his driver's presence, Hunter gently touched his wife's cheek and then pivoted to exit the house. He didn't bother to take cover under the umbrella, preferring instead to run down the walkway to the van's passenger door. Hunter climbed in, and as the driver settled in beside him, Ron peered out the rain-streaked window and absorbed the sight of his wife framed in the open doorway.

To the hypnotic squeak of the van's windshield wipers, they headed north through downtown Silverdale. Traffic was unusually light, and as they passed the Kitsap mall, the driver cleared his throat and broke the constrained silence.

"It's kind of scary what's coming down, huh, sir?"

"That it is, Chief," Hunter succinctly replied.

Several more minutes of silence passed before the enlisted man spoke once again. "Could this thing in Russia really get out of hand and lead to a war, sir?''

Hunter thought a moment before answering. ''I guess that depends on the Russians. All that you can bank on, Chief, is that if they dare make the first aggressive move, we'll be right there to respond to it.''

The rains seemed to further intensify as they continued down Silverdale Way and passed a large sign reading NAVAL SUBMARINE BASE BANGOR: TWO MILES. To get to the main gate, they made a left at the junction of Highway 308. With the wipers barely able to handle the blinding precipitation that fell from the pitch-black sky, the only clue that they were approaching their destination was the appearance of a powerful bank of mercury-vapor lights in the distance. The glowing lights further brightened as they approached the gate itself, and Hunter immediately noted the additional security personnel present. Under normal operating conditions only a single civilian guard would be manning the gate's entryway. This evening the pass and ID gate were heavily guarded, with a pair of tough-looking, rifle-toting marines quick to intercept them as the van braked to a halt in front of the closed steel barricade.

While one of the marines checked the driver, the other sentry approached the van's passenger door. Hunter rolled down the window and handed the guard his plastic identification card. The marine carefully checked the head shot of Hunter embossed on the card, and only after verifying its legitimacy did he return the card and issue a crisp salute.

The barricade swung open and the lights belonging to the base community center soon passed on their right. They turned in the opposite direction and followed the signs leading to the explosives-handling wharf.

The rain continued to fall, and Hunter could barely see the thick evergreen forest that hugged both sides of the road. He knew from an earlier briefing that the base was situated on a plot of nearly seven thousand acres, most of which remained heavily wooded. It was originally developed in 1942 to serve the Pacific theater during World War II as an ammunition storage and loading facility. On February 1, 1977, SUBASE Bangor was officially activated to serve as homeport for the first squadron of Ohio-class Trident submarines.

Less than a mile away from the wharf area, the van was forced to brake to a halt at another barricaded intersection. A trio of marines in full battle dress stood in front of the temporary roadblock that had just been deployed to allow a convoy passage.

Under the ample illumination of a spotlight slung beneath the nose of a hovering helicopter, Hunter watched the convoy cross quickly before them. Leading the way were a pair of HUMVEEs. Each of these rugged utility vehicles had a machine gun mounted on its roof, with a soldier manning it. Close behind the trailing HUMVEE was an armored personnel carrier, with a TOW missile launcher built into its turret. Yet another HUMVEE preceded the camouflaged cab of a large semi pulling a flatbed cargo pallet. Strapped to this pallet was an elongated white cylinder, over thirty-four feet long and six feet in diameter. Hunter didn't have to see any more of the canister to know that inside was a seventy-one-thousand-pound Trident 1 missile.

Hunter's stomach tightened as he recalled this missile's lethal payload. Most likely it was outfitted with eight Mk 4 W-76 nuclear warheads, each of which had a yield of over one hundred kilotons. These warheads would be delivered on a multiple independently targetable reentry vehicle, or MIRV for short, that could hit a target over 4,230 miles distant, within a tenth of a mile circle. Well aware that a Trident submarine carried twenty-four of these incredibly potent weapons, he watched as the taillights belonging to the trailing HUMVEE streaked away.

With the passage of this last vehicle, the marines stepped aside and raised the temporary barricade. The van wasted no time crossing the intersection and completing the short drive down to the water.

The explosives-handling wharf was designed around an immense, multistoried, corrugated steel structure. It was at the landward entrance to this building that the van halted.

"Good luck to you, sir," said the driver as his passenger climbed out of the vehicle.

"Thanks, Chief," Hunter replied, his attention already refocusing on the heavyset, crew-cut petty officer who stood beside the structure's entryway. This individual wore a dark blue USS *Alabama* ball cap, and he alertly stepped out into the rain to greet the newcomer.

"Lieutenant Commander Hunter, I'm Chief Petty Officer John Richter, the *Alabama*'s COB. Captain Ramsey asked me to escort you inside."

Hunter accepted the chief of the boat's firm handshake and followed him through the doorway. A short corridor led them directly into the structure's cavernous interior. Bright overhead floodlights illuminated a scene that never failed to impress Hunter, no matter how many times he saw it. Securely tied to the wharf that the massive building protected was the 560-foot-long, jet black hull of an Ohio-class submarine.

The vessel was in the process of accepting a load of three Trident missiles. The familiar white canisters holding them were being carefully lowered from a ceiling-mounted winch and placed directly over the individual missile tube muzzle doors. They would be subsequently lowered into these tubes, which extended some four stories downward, deep into the hull of the submarine itself.

Quick to note Hunter's interest in the loading process, the COB allowed the officer a moment to absorb the entire scene before beckoning toward the doorway to an adjoining office. Hunter followed him inside, where a single, khaki-clad officer sat behind the room's sole desk, deeply immersed in the contents of a file folder. He was a solidly built Caucasian in his late forties, with short brown, curly hair, a heavily lined forehead, and a serious, no-nonsense persona. Strangely enough, a small Jack Russell terrier was curled up on a tartan blanket behind the officer, and it was this dog who announced their arrival with a single yelp.

"Ah, gentlemen, please have a seat," said the officer, who watched as both Hunter and the COB settled into the pair of straight-backed chairs positioned in front of the desk.

"Lieutenant Commander Hunter, I'm Captain Frank Ramsey, CO of the *Alabama*. I was just reading your personnel jacket."

"Let's see here," he added while readjusting his bifocals and returning his glance to the file folder. "Born and raised in St. Louis, Missouri. A 1978 Naval Academy graduate, with a bachelor of science degree in mechanical engineering—with distinction, I might add. And then there's your master's degree in public administration that you obtained five years ago from the John F. Kennedy School of Government at Harvard."

Looking up from the file at this point, Ramsey met Hunter's gaze and said with a slight grin. "Harvard, Mr. Hunter? I'm impressed."

He returned his glance to Hunter's résumé and continued. "Attended Naval Nuclear Propulsion Program in Idaho, and then reported to the USS *Bremerton*, where you served as chemistry/radiological controls assistant, reactor controls assistant, sonar officer, and weapons officer, all during an extended deployment to the Indian Ocean. In 1982, reported to the Naval Training Center, San Diego for duty as a submarine tactics instructor. After attending the Submarine Officer Advanced course in 1988, you reported to USS *Alaska*, where you made two strategic deterrent patrols as engineering officer. Subsequent assignments brought you to the COMSUBLANT staff, where you served as a junior member of the Nuclear Propulsion Examining Board, and then finally your first XO tours aboard the *Hyman Rickover* and the *Baton Rouge*.

"I also see that you've been awarded the Meritorious Service medal, the Joint Service Commen-

medal, five Navy Commendation awards,
e Navy Achievement medal. You're married,
side with your wife, Julia, and daughter,
in Silverdale.''

ey closed the file and closely examined the
face of the man belonging to this distin-
record. ''I talked to your former CO
ie *Rickover*. He tells me that he tried his
lopt you.''

laughed at this, and Ramsey continued.
no doubt heard, my XO's got appendi-
as the best I've ever had, and now I need
a good man to fill his shoes. And you, Mr. Hunter,
were at the top of the list of prospective candi-
dates.''

''That's nice to know,'' returned Hunter, delighted by the compliment.

''By the way, it's a short list,'' Ramsey retorted,
in all seriousness.

An introspective moment of silence followed.
Hunter did his best to meet Ramsey's piercing stare
directly. Yet he couldn't help but be distracted by
the Jack Russell as it contentedly yawned, oblivious to the unfolding interview.

''Your hobbies, Mr. Hunter,'' Ramsey suddenly
quizzed. ''What do you like to do in your spare
time? Do you paint, play ball, play an instrument,
or ride a motorcycle?''

It took Hunter several seconds to come up with
an answer to this unexpected question. ''I guess
you could say that other than spending most of my
free time with my family, my favorite pastime is
horseback riding.''

Ramsey responded to this while pulling a compact leather cigar case from his pants pocket. "How very interesting. How'd you ever get involved with horses?"

"It was never something that I originally intended to do," remarked Hunter. "In fact, the closest I ever got to a horse was the racetrack, until my wife and I began riding together back in Virginia."

"Western or English?" asked Ramsey.

"Actually, we rode Western," Hunter answered.

Ramsey pulled out a fat cigar from the case and expertly clipped its tapered end before replying. "I find posting extremely painful. It seems to defy all the laws of nature."

Pausing a moment to light his cigar with a gold-ribbed lighter, he added. "What's the best horse you ever rode?"

"I once rode an Arabian," answered Hunter.

Ramsey exhaled a ribbon of fragrant smoke and reflected on it. "Now that's a powerful animal."

"Have you ever ridden an Arabian, Captain?" asked Hunter.

"Are you kidding?" Ramsey snapped. "I can't handle an Arabian. Just give me an ole paint. Horses are fascinating beasts. They're dumb as a post, but very intuitive. In that way, they're not too different from high school girls, who might not have a brain in their head, but do know that all the boys want to screw 'em."

Both Hunter and the COB couldn't help but laugh at this statement, which Ramsey quickly followed up with an additional observation. "Ya know, ya don't hafta be able to read Joyce's *Ulysses* to know where a horse is comin' from. Ya follow me, gents?"

The COB aggressively nodded his head that he did, and while Ramsey went to work on his cigar, Hunter realized that the dog was no longer on its blanket. The brown-and-white terrier had crossed the room, and was curiously sniffing Hunter's crossed leg. He reached down to pet the dog.

"He approves of you," Ramsey observed, while watching the manner in which the dog's tail was wagging. "Jack Russells are the smartest dogs alive. His name's Bear, and he goes everywhere with me."

Ramsey stood, and both Hunter and the COB did likewise. With one hand holding his cigar, Ramsey reached out and shook Hunter's hand.

"Welcome aboard the *Alabama*, son," he said. "Do me proud."

"Thank you, sir," returned Hunter. "I will."

The COB offered their new XO a handshake as well, adding, "Congratulations, Lieutenant Commander Hunter."

Not to be denied, Bear issued a terse congratulatory yelp of his own. And once again the alien sound of laughter filled the previously tense confines of the sparsely furnished room.

It was well after midnight when Vladimir Radchenko finally completed the last meeting of a day that had started shortly after sunrise. Though totally exhausted and in great need of a few precious hours of sound sleep, he decided to stretch his cramped limbs with a brief walk.

He left the train car where his temporary headquarters had been set up and headed at once into the surrounding woods. He was able to forget about the two armed soldiers who religiously followed him into the tree line the moment he passed the first copse of tall spruces.

The fresh Siberian air was like a tonic, and he gratefully filled his lungs, ignoring the fact that the temperature was below freezing. Remembering well the last time that he had been able to take such a hike while visiting his dacha outside of Moscow, Radchenko peered up into the crystal clear night sky.

A full moon commanded the heavens. Yet despite its bright glow, a myriad of stars were readily visible. He looked on in wonder as a shooting star streaked overhead, and went over in his mind the incredible, history-making events of the last few days. This whirlwind of activity had been all set in motion the moment he left his dacha and and boarded the helicopter for the short flight to Moscow.

With both Viktor Sorokin and Boris Arbatov faithfully at his flanks, he brazenly stormed up to the Parliament's podium and announced the beginning of their revolution. As anticipated, their poor, feeble president overreacted to this declaration, immediately disbanding Parliament and declaring martial law.

With political momentum and the will of an enraged people on their side, Radchenko's followers rose in revolt throughout the length and breadth of their beloved country. To consolidate their rising power, Radchenko and his advisors boarded an Antonov An-22 transport to begin the long flight to Vladivostok. Here they joined up with thousands of loyal troops anxious to be the first military unit to take a stand and carry the banner of their proud movement into battle.

Radchenko was right there with the troops when they easily overran the defenses of their immediate military objective and took control of the vital base, a victory which earned him the respect of an entire planet. No longer would the world look upon his movement as a joke, an aberration, an assembly of outdated fools. Now they had real power, and their haughty enemies now understood real fear.

Quickly stifling a yawn, Radchenko knew that the next few days would be of great importance to the ultimate success of their cause. As the long day started overcoming him, the fifty-nine-year-old politician decided it was time to return to the train.

The renewed urge for a cigarette betokened his weariness as he stepped out of the woods and spotted several figures huddled alongside the railroad siding. Even from a distance, Radchenko could recognize the tall, dignified former minister of defense, Viktor Sorokin. As he approached them, he saw that another of the group was a woman, and a damn attractive one at that. Her two male companions held video equipment.

"So there you are, Vladimir Ilyich," greeted Viktor with great relief. "I'm glad that we were able to catch up with you before you retired for the night."

"I was only taking my customary evening constitutional, Viktor," said Radchenko, doing his best to give his step more spring to impress the woman. He disliked even his wife seeing him tired. "Now, how can I be of service to you?"

"Comrade Radchenko," boldly interjected the female in a peculiar dialect of English, "I'm Sarah Turkannon of the Australian Broadcasting Company. I'm sorry that we missed this afternoon's scheduled interview, but our flight was delayed and we only just got here. I realize the late hour, but would you mind answering a few questions? I've been guaranteed a worldwide video pickup, and I promise to take up only a couple of minutes of your valuable time."

Well aware of the priceless publicity value of such a television interview, and equally aware of the attractive reporter's ample bustline, Radchenko graciously assented. They decided to conduct the interview inside the train car. Fortified with a healthy snifter of brandy, Radchenko peered into the bright lights of the video camera with a look mixing grim determination and weariness. Exhaustion, when used correctly, did have its virtues.

"This is Sarah Turkannon, coming to you live from a train siding, somewhere north of Vladivostok. With me this evening is Vladimir Radchenko, the complex, often misunderstood leader of Russia's Ultra-Nationalist Party . . ."

Amongst the hundreds of millions of television sets that this broadcast eventually reached, was one located inside the wardroom of the USS *Alabama*. Currently gathered around the twenty-seven-inch monitor screen, intently watching the interview on prerecorded videotape, were five of the Trident submarine's officers, including Lieutenant Peter Ince, the vessel's weapons officer, and known to his shipmates simply as Weps.

The slightly built, African-American weapons officer was in the process of cleaning a smudge of icing off the lenses of his wire rims. This icing came from the piece of birthday cake he was busy gobbling. After he received the call sending him scurrying back to the *Alabama*, Julie, Robin's mother, had thoughtfully wrapped it up for him.

The interview had been playing for several minutes, and Ince watched as the pretty Aussie reporter tried hard to hide her shock, while interpreting the answer to a question that she had just asked.

". . . so what you're saying is, if Russian nationals were harmed . . ."

"No!" shouted the dynamic individual whom she was interviewing.

With this invective, the television screen filled with a close-up of Vladimir Radchenko. There could be no missing the heavy dark circles that shadowed the revolutionary's bloodshot eyes as he passionately continued.

"What I'm saying, Comrade Turkannon, is if one Russian citizen is killed by outside elements while I'm president, I will kill nine hundred thousand of those people responsible."

The young reporter instinctively gasped at the sheer vehement force of this reply. Her blouse momentarily heaved upward, and the dark-haired officer seated to the right of Ince forcefully cried out.

"Oh, my God!" exclaimed Lieutenant Billy Linkletter, the sub's tactical systems operator in charge of all conventional weapons. "Chop, stop the tape! Play that portion back!"

Bob Dougherty, whose nickname came from the pork chop–shaped supply officer insignia that graced his collar, rewound the tape to repeat the scene. "What in the hell are you carrying on about, Linkletter?" asked Chop, pushing the play button.

As the reporter gasped Linkletter explained himself. "Jesus H. Christ! Look at the size of those tits buried beneath that blouse!"

A roar of laughter filled the wardroom. Yet as the taped interview resumed, Roy Zimmer, the boat's communications officer, disgustedly spoke out. "Come on, guys, pipe down!"

As the snickering laughter in the wardroom finally faded, Sarah Turkannon's concerned voice once more prevailed. "I don't believe that you quite understand the effect of such talk."

"My dear young lady," interrupted Vladimir

Radchenko, a fierce gleam glowing in his eyes, "I do not engage in mere talk. These are serious threats that I'm uttering, threats that I'll very shortly be in a position to carry out!"

During the brief pause that followed, Darik Westerguard, the sub's sonar officer, blurted out, "Damn, that guy's psycho!"

All of them watched breathlessly as Radchenko leaned forward and continued. "If you'd like an example of just such a threat that I'll shortly be acting on, you only have to look as far as the nearby Kuril Islands. As far as I'm concerned, these islands are the rightful property of the Russian people, occupied by us since 1945. And if the Japanese, or any other power, dares to claim them, we shall put our great navy to sea and encircle the Kurils. And if anybody should make a move against us, I will hit them with a barrage of nuclear weapons!"

It was at that moment that the wardroom door unexpectedly swung open. Captain Frank Ramsey stormed into the compartment, followed by Rear Admiral Mike Williams, the admiral's aide, Lieutenant Commander Ron Hunter, and the *Alabama*'s COB.

The arrival of a flag officer in their midst caused the seated officers to snap to their feet. They watched as Ramsey and the admiral made their way to the head of the rectangular table. While the admiral's aide set up the tripod that he had brought along and removed a large, cardboard-backed map from his flat leather portfolio, both Hunter and the COB took positions to the immediate right of the two senior officers.

It was Ramsey who silently signaled his men to

be seated. He also nodded toward the blaring television, whose screen was again filled with a head shot of Radchenko, and made a gesture across his throat with his right hand. Chop was quick to take the hint. He picked up the remote control to stop the tape and turn off the set.

"I take it that you've seen enough of our dear Comrade, Vladimir Radchenko," said Ramsey facetiously. "Gentlemen, after a nice little vacation, it looks like we're back at it again. So I hope you enjoyed the short peace, because as of this moment, we're back in business."

With his determined gaze scanning the rapt faces of his men, Ramsey continued. "During the good ole days of the Cold War, the Russians could always be counted on to do whatever was in their best interest. But this Radchenko's playin' a whole new ball game, with a whole new set of rules. Now we've all heard politicians talk before. But I don't think this man's talkin' just to get his picture in the paper. I think he's got a serious weed up his ass and a legitimate gripe as well, always a dangerous combination. And I think he's capable of doin' every goddamn thing he said he'll do. That's why we have to go out there and give the man a moment of pause. So ends theory. Thus let us begin the facts. Admiral Williams . . ."

The distinguished, grey-haired commander of Submarine Group 17 took over the briefing at this point. "We have been informed by the NSA that an entire corps of the Russian Army is involved in the rebel takeover. That's four armored divisions, numbering sixty thousand men. Their ranks continue to swell as Radchenko wins the hearts and minds of thousands of defecting Russian soldiers.''

The admiral grasped a telescoping, metallic pointer from his aide, and approached the tripod. Displayed there was a detailed topographic map showing Vladivostok and the territory that surrounded the port city.

''The brunt of the rebel attack appears to be focused here, at the strategic missile base at Art'om.'' Admiral Williams pointed out an area just north of Vladivostok, and added, ''This base is home to twenty-five hardened silos, housing the SS-18 intercontinental ballistic missile. As you very well know, the SS-18 is the largest ICBM in the Russian inventory. Each missile is capable of holding up to eight MIRV'd warheads, with a yield of two megatons apiece, and an effective range of well over seven thousand miles. Thus, they could easily reach the American West Coast, or come in over the North Pole to take out Washington and New York.''

''I think it's also important to note that these rebels have also gained control of Art'om's naval facility,'' Ramsey interjected. ''Preliminary SOSUS data shows that four Akula-class attack subs surged into the Pacific from this site shortly after the rebel takeover.''

''Admiral Williams,'' dared Chop from the opposite end of the wardroom table. ''Can Radchenko's forces really launch these ICBMs?''

The admiral somberly glanced at Ramsey before replying. ''Good question, Lieutenant. As of this moment, the legitimate Russian government assures us that negotiations are under way with the rebels, and that Radchenko's forces definitely do not possess those missile launch codes.''

A collective gasp of relief escaped the lips of the *Alabama*'s junior officers. Ramsey was quick to pick up on it, and he added forcefully, ''As far as I'm concerned, any reassurances on the part of the Russian government don't mean squat. If Radchenko's able to get this far, there's no doubt in my mind that he's capable of cracking those release codes.''

''That's why the commander-in-chief, through the National Military Command Authority, has directed U.S. military forces to immediately set a defense condition of DEFCON Four,'' the admiral informed them.

Ramsey capped this sobering news by revealing their orders. ''We have been directed to get under way tomorrow at 0700 hours. We'll be assuming alert coverage, mid-Pacific, of the Far Eastern TVD target package, that includes Art'om and its environs.''

Briefly checking to see if Admiral Williams had anything else to say, Ramsey readdressed his men. ''Lieutenant Commander Hunter is your new XO. Please bring him up to speed on the ship's personnel and our supply situation. Now, are there any more questions?''

Dead silence prevailed, and Ramsey nodded. ''Very good, gentlemen. Please inform the men of our situation. That is all.''

Without another word spoken, Ramsey crisply led Rear Admiral Williams, his aide, and the *Alabama*'s COB out of the wardroom. This left Hunter behind with his five new shipmates.

''Damn, DEFCON Four!'' Chop exclaimed.

"I told you that Radchenko's a psycho," Darik Westerguard said. "That fool's gonna start a friggin' world war!"

"Not if we can help it," Hunter replied firmly.

Suddenly remembering the new man in their midst, Weps graciously initiated the proper introductions. "Guys, let me be the first to welcome our new XO aboard. Hell, Ron Hunter's only bailed my ass out about six, seven hundred times."

Hunter grinned, and Weps beckoned toward the heavyset, balding figure seated at the far end of the table. "Bobby Dougherty is our supply officer. Just don't bad talk the Celtics or Red Sox, XO, and Chop will make sure we don't run out of Joe."

As Hunter traded nods with the amiable supply officer, Weps addressed the blond-haired officer seated on Chop's right. "Billy Linkletter's our TSO. A word of warning, XO. Keep the horny bastard away from Julia, and whatever you do, don't give him your sister's phone number."

The men laughed, and Weps went on to introduce Darik Westerguard and Roy Zimmer before adding, "Just so you know the score, Ron and I served together on the *Baton Rouge*."

"I'm certain that was an experience that you'll never forget," said Chop to Hunter, the barest of Boston accents gracing his words. "So, XO, what do you think of the old man?"

Hunter answered as honestly as possible. "If you're referring to Captain Ramsey, I like him."

"You really like him?" repeated Weps with disbelief.

Hunter nodded. "It's odd, but Ramsey manages

to intimidate you and put you at ease, all at the very same time.''

''That's him, all right,'' agreed the sub's sonar officer.

''You know, I think that it was his dog who gave me the final seal of approval,'' Hunter offered.

''The skipper's certainly weird about that mutt,'' Chop said. ''He takes him everywhere, even on patrol, and has me order him special dog food.''

''Hell, I hear the skipper considers Bear his personal good luck charm,'' Linkletter added.

''Whatever,'' said Chop. ''But the navy looks the other way, because it's Ramsey.''

Lieutenant Zimmer proudly chimed in. ''He's one of the few skippers left who have actually seen combat. He took SEALs into Panama in '89 and fired Tomahawks in the Gulf in '91.''

''And don't forget Ramsey's burning down of nine XOs in 1995,'' Westerguard joked.

The men laughed, prompting Weps to grab the right side of his abdomen and sarcastically groan. ''And that's not counting the one he lost to appendicitis!''

Another round of laughter filled the wardroom. Hunter joined in, though his joviality was clearly forced.

The sub's communications officer sensed Hunter's apparent unease, and Zimmer did his best to assuage any second thoughts that Hunter might have. ''When you pull a patrol with a skipper like Ramsey, especially with all this shit that's goin' down, it can make your career.''

''Or break it,'' said Weps, no joke intended.

Hunter couldn't help but catch the seriousness of

Ince's response. His shipmates were likewise affected. There was a noticeable loss of levity as their new XO looked at his watch and then began discussing the myriad of details that would have to be attended to, so the *Alabama* could meet its ordered sailing time.

The dawn broke clear and cool. For Ron Hunter, the short night had afforded him little actual sleep. He was content merely to lie in bed with his wife firmly in his embrace, soaking in her touch and scent, and trying hard to sort out the tangled thoughts that rushed through his mind.

Regardless of the fact that he was a veteran submariner who had endured his fair share of ninety-day deterrence patrols, the last night spent ashore was always hard on him. This was especially the case during the restless evening just past. Current world events didn't make things any easier, and Hunter did his best to hide his gathering anxieties from his family.

He got up long before his wife and daughter, and quietly slipped into the bathroom to shower and shave. It was still pitch-black outside as he entered the kitchen and squeezed a pitcher of fresh orange juice, prepared some French toast, and flicked on the coffeemaker. Only then did he go to awaken Julia and Robin.

The first hint of dawn was just coloring the eastern horizon as they ate their breakfast together, then reluctantly climbed into the car for the short ride to the sub base. Not long after backing out of the driveway Robin curled up asleep in the back-seat and a contemplative silence prevailed as they sped over the deserted streets of Silverdale and continued northward.

Ever thankful that the rains had finally stopped, they were all too soon passing through the navy base's main gate. Security remained tight, and Hunter had to display the proper I.D. card for each of his two dependents.

The morning was turning out to be a glorious one. A powdery blue sky stretched for as far as the eye could see, and the thick pine forest that hugged the road leading to the pier was sparkling fresh from the recent rains.

A steep incline led to the entrance to the pier, and it was there they encountered dozens of parked vehicles. These automobiles, pickup trucks, and vans belonged to the families of the *Alabama*'s crew. Since only crew members were allowed onto Delta pier itself, many a tearful good-bye was taking place right alongside the sloping roadway.

Hunter was fortunate to find a place to park at the very bottom of the hill, almost directly across from the last security checkpoint. He turned off the ignition and turned to face his wife, who appeared to be watching his each and every move.

"You make certain to come back to me, sailor, you hear?" she sadly whispered, the tears welling in her dark eyes.

Fighting his own gathering tears, Hunter reached for Julia and hugged her tightly. As never before, he felt the intensity of their love for each other.

Having met during college, and married only days after graduation, they had spent the majority of their adult lives together. What kind of life had it been for her, though, with him gone a good six months out of every year? Whereas a good many submarine marriages ended in divorce, their relationship only seemed to tighten with each year's passing. It only went to prove what a remarkable woman he had picked to fall in love with.

As their lips finally touched, a sleepy voice from the backseat broke the erotic spell. "Hey, you guys, remember me?"

Hunter pulled back his head, and turned to face his daughter. "I'll never forget you, squirt. How about giving Daddy a big hug?"

Robin readily stood on the backseat and tightly squeezed Hunter by the neck. She lovingly kissed her father's cheek, and Julia leaned over and joined them for a communal hug.

It was the sonorous bellow of a powerful air horn that broke up their joint embrace. Hunter ruffled his daughter's hair, affectionately touched his wife's smooth cheek, and, after checking his digital watch, got out of the car.

Dozens of sailors scurried past him on their way to the ramp leading to Delta pier. After extracting his seabag from the trunk, he returned to his family for a final good-bye. By this time Julia had scooted over behind the steering wheel and Robin had climbed over to replace her in the passenger seat.

It was as Hunter was planting a final kiss on his wife's forehead that a portly, mustached sailor dressed in the khaki uniform of a chief petty officer walked up to their car.

"Excuse me," he casually said. "Lieutenant Commander Hunter, sir?"

Hunter looked up into the sailor's kind face, and warmly grinned. "Well, I'll be. If it isn't the best master machinist in the entire U.S. Navy. It's good to see you again, Chief Marichek. Damn, how long's it been?"

Rick Marichek started to count off the years on his fingers, but prematurely terminated this mental effort. "Ever since our last patrol together aboard the *Rickover*, sir. When I heard yesterday that we drew you as our new XO, I just couldn't wait to say hello."

The overweight petty officer politely nodded toward Julia, yet diverted his glance when three of his shipmates, with duffel bags draped over their shoulders, passed by the car.

"Hey, guys!" he shouted. "Come meet our new XO."

The dungaree-clad trio shyly walked over to the car, and Marichek readily initiated the introductions. "Lieutenant Commander Hunter, I'd like you to meet three very special members of the *Alabama*'s crew. Chief Howard Rono here is our cook, and a goodly portion of this spare tire I'm carryin' around my waist attests to his culinary talents. Russell Vossler is our resident radio whiz, and Petty Officer First Class Danny Rivetti is one of the best sonar operators in Bangor."

Before Hunter could shake their hands, the air horn sounded once more. Chief Marichek and his shipmates took this as the urgent summons it was and excused themselves for the pier.

"I don't know, Julia," said Hunter to his wife,

before leaving her with a final kiss. "But these kids I've been going to sea with lately seem to be gettin' younger with each and every patrol!"

When he was finally able to wrench himself away from the car, there could be no missing the tears that were freely falling down his wife's face. A tightness was gathering deep in his gut as he passed by the security barricade and began his way down the long ramp leading to Delta pier.

With each successive step, he was putting additional distance between normal, everyday existence and the hidden, arcane world of the submariner. From now on there'd be no phone calls or letters home. If they were lucky, and conditions allowed it, perhaps they'd be able to receive a brief "familygram" message from their loved ones, though that would be the extent of their outside contact.

Hunter dared not look back. He increased his stride and instead focused his attention forward. Beyond the sparkling waters of the Hood Canal lay the lush green forested shores of the Olympic peninsula. The snowcapped Olympic mountains beckoned in the distance, and Hunter inhaled a deep lungful of crisp fresh air. Already the pull of the outside world was weakening, and he redirected his eyes to the unique triangular structure that was his immediate destination.

Officially known as the Delta support facility, the refit pier was positioned 400 feet away from shore, so that the Tridents could directly approach their tie-up berths without a channel having to be constantly dredged. The refit pier was shaped in the form of a modified letter A. Each of its 700-foot-long legs could service an individual submarine.

The leg paralleling the shoreline contained a 90-foot-wide by 700-foot-long dry dock. This dry dock was the deepest in the U.S. Navy at 63 feet, and had a 16-foot-thick concrete floor.

From his current position on the ramp leading to the pier, Hunter could readily view the 58,000-square-foot support building sitting in the middle of the structure. As he remembered from his initial briefing upon arriving in Bangor, this incredibly engineered pier was one of the first of its kind built upon individual pilings to allow fingerling salmon free access while transiting the Hood Canal. The mere attempt to address such an environmental concern demonstrated the navy's sincere commitment to the area's ecological preservation.

Of course, the very reason for Delta pier's existence soon became evident as Hunter got an excellent bow-on view of the USS *Alabama*. The 560-foot-long, black-hulled Trident was tied up at refit pier number one. An American flag proudly flapped from its sail-mounted pole, while dozens of sailors were in the process of boarding the vessel from an elevated brow located just aft of the fairwater. Hunter's pulse proudly quickened with this sighting, and with the outside world all but a distant memory now, he anxiously approached his new home.

The first portion of the *Alabama* to pass on his left was the boat's teardrop-shaped bow. It was there that the vessel's immense sonar sphere was located. Hunter spotted a thin, frothing white line of bubbles alongside the rounded bow, and he determined the source of this disturbance as a wet-suited SCUBA diver suddenly surfaced beside the pier. Such divers were usually members of the sub's crew, and were sent below to check the hull for possible limpet mines, sonic pingers, or any other irregularities.

Hunter encountered a long line of enlisted men stretching from the pier to the brow and finally ending at the sub's aft access trunk. This human daisy chain was in the process of loading last-minute supplies under the vigilant eye of Lieutenant Dougherty.

"Take care with that box, Barnes!" shouted Chop to the young sailor on the first step of the brow. "Those are eggs in there, son!"

Chop greeted Hunter with a warm smile. "Welcome, XO. Me and the boys are just loading the perishables."

Any reply on Hunter's part was cut short by Seaman Barnes, who managed to drop the next carton that was handed to him. Hunter tried his best not to laugh as hundreds of potatoes burst from the split cardboard and rolled out onto the pier.

As the embarrassed sailor and his shipmates went to their hands and knees to clean up the mess, Captain Frank Ramsey emerged from the aft access trunk. Following him up onto the deck from the bowels of the *Alabama* were the boat's COB and several junior officers. Ramsey disgustedly grunted upon spotting the sailors involved in the potato cleanup, and there was a definite sharpness to his glance upon spotting Hunter standing on the pier, with his seabag in hand.

"So glad that you could make it this morning, Mr. Hunter," greeted Ramsey. "Have one of the crew stow your gear below. Right now, I'd like you to arrange assembling the entire crew pierside in ten minutes' time."

With the invaluable assistance of the COB, Hunter was able to fulfill the captain's difficult request with a whole thirty seconds to spare. Except for a skeleton engineering watch that remained on the boat, the *Alabama*'s 150 officers, chiefs, and enlisted men neatly formed their ranks on the pier, directly facing the submarine. The Stars and Stripes crisply flapped from the sail as Ramsey, Hunter, and the COB faced this assembly.

"Place the crew at parade rest, COB," Ramsey instructed.

"Crew, parade rest!" ordered the portly chief of the boat.

With eyes forward and their hands cocked behind their backs, the crew listened as Ramsey addressed them.

"I have a few words to say before we get under way. As all of you know, there's trouble in Russia. So they called on us. And we're going over there with the most lethal killing machine ever devised by the hand of man. We are capable of launching more firepower than has ever been released in the entire history of war for one purpose only—to keep our country free. We constitute both the front line and the last line of defense. Thus I expect and demand your best. Anything less, and you should have joined the air force."

The crew broke out into laughter with this last remark. From his position two steps behind Ramsey and slightly to his left, Hunter also laughed, as did the COB, who stood to the XO's right.

"This might be our commander-in-chief's Navy,

but it's my boat," Ramsey continued. "And you might be your mothers' sons, but now you're my boys. And all I ask is that you keep up with me. If you can't, that strange sensation you'll be feeling in the seat of your pants will be my boot in your ass."

"COB!" he forcefully shouted, without looking behind him.

"Yes, sir!" the COB retorted.

"You are aware of the name of this ship, aren't you, COB?" quizzed Ramsey.

The COB was quick to reply. "Very aware, sir!"

"It bears a proud name, doesn't it, COB?" Ramsey continued, with ever-rising intensity.

"Very proud, sir!" said the COB.

"And it represents millions of fine people."

The COB nodded. "Fine people, sir!"

"Who live in a fine, outstanding state."

"Outstanding, sir!"

"In the greatest country in the entire world!"

"In the entire world, sir!"

"And what is that name, COB?" asked Ramsey without missing a beat.

"*Alabama*, sir!"

"And what do we say?" Ramsey questioned, his eyes glowing with pride.

"Go '*Bama*!" returned the COB as he looked at the crew and nodded.

"Roll Tide!" exclaimed the men in unison.

Hunter couldn't help but find himself emotionally stimulated by this exchange. Surely it was a private ritual, the by-product of past patrols and relationships, the nature of which the sub's new XO was just now getting a glimpse.

"COB, call the crew to attention," Ramsey ordered, his tone all business.

"Aye, aye, sir," said the COB. "Crew, attention! Department heads, take charge. Man the maneuvering watch."

With a final flurry, the men broke ranks and scurried toward the brow. Hunter stepped aside to let them pass, still strangely affected by the unexpected ritual that he had just witnessed.

To reach the sheltering depths of the Pacific the *Alabama* had to endure a 150-mile-long surface transit. The first leg of this route would take them almost due north up the tranquil waters of the Hood Canal.

But first Hunter had to coordinate the crew's efforts as the final mooring line was cast off and the harbor tugs arrived to pull them away from Delta pier.

Unable even to find a spare moment to slip into his poopy suit, the comfortable, blue coveralls that officers and enlisted men alike preferred to wear while at sea, Hunter all too soon found himself being called to the top of the sail by the captain. Hunter accessed the three-story-high sail, also known as the fairwater, by way of a steep, vertical ladder located just forward of the control room. He climbed past a phone-talker, assigned to man the fairwater's interior hatch, and, with a bit of difficulty, finally reached the sail's exterior bridge.

Lieutenants Zimmer and Linkletter were the current members of the bridge's maneuvering watch. Hunter was just able to squeeze in between them. They greeted him with a nod, and Hunter watched as the sub's TSO relayed their latest course bearing from below, while Zimmer used a red wax pencil to record this bearing on the perspex windshield that was set up on the bridge's forward lip.

A brilliant blue sky stretched overhead. The air was fresh, and Hunter looked over the surging sphere of water that was bubbling over their bow and viewed the rapidly approaching Hood Canal bridge. The mid-portion of this floating structure had already been removed in anticipation of their transit. A good number of cars were parked on the span, and Hunter assumed that many of the women and children gathered alongside the bridge's railing had family members aboard the *Alabama* and had purposely assembled there for one last good-bye.

"Looks like we really lucked out with this weather," broke a familiar, gruff voice from behind.

Hunter turned around and immediately spotted the speaker of these words. The *Alabama*'s commanding officer stood on the top portion of the sail, directly behind the indented bridge. He wore a short khaki jacket and had one hand on the temporarily rigged steel enclosure known as the playpen. A lookout stood behind Ramsey, with the vessel's periscope, induction and radar masts occupying the rear portion of the fairwater.

"Please join me, Mr. Hunter," Ramsey casually invited.

Hunter climbed up into the playpen. From that elevated vantage point he had a superb view of both the powerful wake constantly streaming over their bow and the gayly waving crowds assembled on the floating bridge.

Ramsey removed two cigars from his breast

pocket and, after clipping their tapered ends, handed one to Hunter.

"Here," said Ramsey, as he pulled out a lighter. "It's all part of your qualifications for command."

Hunter didn't dare refuse this offer. He allowed Ramsey to light his cigar and tentatively inhaled. The tobacco was smoother than he expected, with a rich, smoky taste.

"Ah, my last breath of polluted air for the next sixty-five days," reflected Ramsey, appreciatively puffing away on his own cigar. "I'm gonna miss it."

Hunter laughed and Ramsey added, "Hell, I don't trust air I can't see."

They were in the process of passing through the bridge now. Ramsey made it a point to wave to the crowds gathered on both sides of them.

"Sound the air horn, Mr. Zimmer," he instructed.

Their communications officer passed the order down to the control room and, seconds later, a deep, resonant blast shook the air. Again Ramsey waved to the crowd of onlookers, many of whom were children.

"I don't suppose that your wife and child are part of that crowd?" said Ramsey, as he gestured toward the bridge that they were already leaving behind them.

Hunter exhaled a long ribbon of cigar smoke before replying. "I doubt it, sir. Good-byes are hard enough on my Julia, and she's most likely home by now."

"My wife was the same way," Ramsey revealed. "Just kicked me out of the door and couldn't even bear driving me down to the pier.''

Hunter grunted. "I didn't realize that you were married, Captain. Any children?''

"Not that I know of,'' replied Ramsey bitterly. "I'm divorced. And she went on to marry the skipper of a goddamn frigate.''

"At least she kept it in the navy, sir,'' Hunter offered.

"Hell,'' spit Ramsey with the barest of grins. "It was the goddamn navy that kept it in her!''

Both of them laughed, and long moments of contemplative silence followed. Hunter was genuinely surprised to find himself enjoying his cigar. He also couldn't help but enjoy his current company. Though a bit eccentric and rough around the edges, Captain Frank Ramsey emitted the pure command qualities that Hunter hoped to master someday. The *Alabama*'s CO was formed out of the same ingredients that legends were made of, and Hunter knew that he was extremely fortunate to have gotten this unexpected call to duty.

He momentarily lost his thoughts in the powerful dome of water that constantly spewed over their bow, and contentedly puffed away on his cigar. It was a soaring gull that diverted his attention to the deep blue sky overhead. On both sides of the canal thick evergreen pines hugged the uninhabited shores, with man's presence limited to an infrequent fishing cabin. Beyond the pine forest the majestic snowcapped peaks of the Olympic mountain range prevailed. They would be entering Puget Sound shortly, and then the *Alabama* would turn west, for the hundred-mile transit of the Strait of Juan de Fuca. And only after that transit was completed would the *Alabama* be submerging to travel the black depths of its intended medium.

The monotonous roar of the bow wake merged with the powerful, muted rumble of their engines, producing an almost hypnotic effect. The *Alabama*'s single, massive propeller bit into the clear water, and Hunter was barely aware of the slight rocking of the keelless ship beneath him.

Belowdeck the crew would be busy adjusting to a world that knew no night or day. From now on, the total reason for their existence would be to service the incredibly complex machine that provided their home. An incredible amount of work awaited Hunter in the days ahead as he tried his best to become one with this crew, and to earn their trust.

"Bravo, Mr. Hunter," said Ramsey, his gruff voice totally unexpected.

"Excuse me, sir?" returned Hunter, his thoughts elsewhere.

"You knew to shut up and enjoy the view," Ramsey explained. "Most eggheads want to talk it away. As far as I'm concerned, your stock just went up a couple of points."

Hunter's chest swelled with pride. "Thank you, sir."

"Son," said Ramsey, without shifting his glance off the bow wake, "there's an old saying that people who marry for money, at the end of the day, earn every goddamn penny. Any benefit you get from this patrol you'll have earned. But allow me to offer a tiny bit of advice. If you want your own boat someday, the very worst thing you can do is worry about yourself or try to impress me. I can't stand a save-ass, and I won't abide a kiss-ass. You just keep your priorities straight—your mission and your men.''

Halting to take a puff on his cigar, Ramsey looked at his XO. "How do you like that cigar, son?"

Caught in mid-puff himself, Hunter started to talk before clearing all of the smoke from his lungs, and he broke out in a fit of coughing as a result. "It's good, sir," he managed.

Ramsey grinned. "Your first?"

"Yes, it is, sir," admitted Hunter.

"Well, don't like 'em too much, XO. These Monte Cristo number twos are more expensive than drugs."

Admiralty Inlet was passing to port, and with their arrival into the crowded waters of Puget Sound, they had a great deal more surface traffic to contend with. The majority of these vessels were fishing trawlers or pleasure boats, though an immense, pallet-laden container ship was in the process of rounding Port Townsend.

Lieutenant Zimmer formulated a course that would keep them well out of this ship's way. Ramsey approved it and took a moment to peer up into the clear heavens.

"I guess now's as good a time as any to wave good-bye to Ivan," he offered.

In response to this lighthearted remark, both Ramsey and his communications officer raised their right fists overhead and extended their middle fingers.

"That should give that bastard Radchenko something to think about when he monitors the next satellite uplink,'' said Ramsey. "To be an effective deterrent, everyone has to know that you're there!''

Hunter nodded in agreement, and he watched as Ramsey suddenly tossed his cigar overboard. With a detached coolness he then excused himself to go below, leaving Hunter on the bridge to see them safely into the Strait of Juan de Fuca.

Eight hours after shoving off from Delta pier, the USS *Alabama* finally reached open water and was ready to submerge. Hunter had long since left his post on the bridge, and while the sub had transited the straits westward, he'd been able to spend some time in his new stateroom stowing away his gear.

Though many landlubbers would consider his quarters incredibly cramped, Hunter felt otherwise. Of all the members of the crew, only he and the captain had a private stateroom. Though it wasn't much bigger than Julia's closet back home, it was large enough to contain a fold-up bed, a work desk, Pullman-style sink, and an adequate amount of storage space for his gear. A doorway set into the forward bulkhead led directly to the head that he shared with the boat's CO. It was during his first visit to the head that he realized that he'd also be sharing this space with their "unofficial" crew member. A wicker basket with a tartan pad was positioned beside the sink, this being Bear's bunk space.

It was with great relief that Hunter stripped off his khakis and slipped into his poopy suit. After taking some time to visit the wardroom and grab a grilled turkey and cheese sandwich and some to-mato soup, he returned to his quarters to complete his unpacking. He stowed away the rest of his clothing and spent most of his time organizing his desk. With a framed picture of Julia and Robin stra-tegically placed on the wall in front of him, he inventoried his office supplies and began sorting through the stack of paperwork that awaited his at-tention.

Weps dropped by to visit him while he was in the midst of this time-consuming chore. He helped Hunter put a dent in the two-foot-high stack by picking out the correspondence that needed the XO's immediate attention. Hunter was then able to push aside the stack of technical manuals and junk mail that remained, to attend to at a later date.

It was while examining the latest chemistry read-ings of their reactor that he was informed that the boat was ready to dive. He immediately pushed aside his paperwork and exited his stateroom. A short flight of stairs conveyed him up to the boat's first level, and he entered the control room just as Lieutenant Westerguard was in the process of climbing down through the hatch that led to the sail.

"Chief of the watch," informed the breathless sonar officer, "last man's down from the bridge. Hatch is secured. Bridge is rigged for dive."

The chief of the watch repeated this information, and Hunter crossed the control room to join the captain on the periscope pedestal. From this slightly elevated platform at the after end of the equipment-packed compartment, he had a clear view of the entire room.

Facing forward and looking from left to right, Hunter scanned the brightly lit compartment that was approximately the same size as a two-car garage. He surveyed the massive ballast control panel, where the chief of the watch monitored the buttons and switches that governed the boat's ballast and trim tanks. It was the chief of the watch who caused the boat to dive, surface, or remain neutrally buoyant. To the immediate right of his panel was the diving control console. Two young enlisted men sat behind the aircraft-style steering yokes that operated the diving planes and rudder. Seated between them was the COB, their current diving officer.

The COB had the stub of an unlit cigar clenched between his lips. The heavyset, senior enlisted man had his eyes locked on the variety of glowing digital indicator panels set into the console directly before him. The readouts showed their current heading, depth, and dive angle.

"Quartermaster, sounding?" requested Ramsey, from his position beside Hunter on the pedestal.

"Sounding eight-five fathoms, sir," returned the quartermaster, who was stationed alongside the navigation plot in the aft starboard portion of the control room.

"Very well, COB, submerge the ship," Ramsey ordered.

"Submerge the ship, aye, Captain," repeated the COB, who next addressed the petty officer manning the diving console. "Chief of the watch, pass the word over the 1MC, Dive, Dive. Sound two blasts on the diving alarm.''

Hunter noted a definite calmness in the manner in which the control room team went about their work. This said a lot about the management style of the *Alabama*'s current skipper. Whereas many COs that Hunter had served under liked to micromanage their crews to such an extent that one could actually feel the tension in the air during difficult transition periods such as diving, Ramsey led with a minimum of interference. As a result, his men displayed a high confidence level, which helped solidify them into a team.

''Dive! Dive!'' shouted the chief of the watch into his intercom handset. He followed up his announcement to the crew by reaching up to the top portion of the diving console and activating the diving alarm.

A blaring Klaxon sounded throughout the ship, and Hunter watched the chief of the watch readdress his console to open the vessel's vents. A series of green circles lit up the digital display, indicating that these vents were indeed now open, and that the ballast tanks were filling with tons of onrushing seawater.

''Helm, make your depth eight-five feet. Ten degree down angle, at one-third speed,'' instructed Ramsey.

COB repeated this order, and the planesman pushed down on his yoke to engage the stern diving planes. Soon the deck of the *Alabama* would be awash, and Hunter shifted his attention to one of the platform's two periscopes.

A quick peek through the eyepiece of the Mk 18

search scope showed that they had these seas all to themselves. A light chop prevailed topside, with an occasional swell lapping up against the scope's oblong viewing lens.

As Hunter was in the midst of a 360-degree scan, his attention was drawn to the western horizon. There the dusk sky was aglow with brilliant bands of red, orange, and yellow. It was a stimulating sight, and Hunter took this spectacular sunset at sea as an excellent omen of things to come.

Their next ordered depth change took them one hundred feet below the Pacific's surface. The periscope was useless here, and Hunter engaged a lever that sent the stainless steel scope casing sliding back down into the protective sail. With this simple act, no further sign of the vessel's presence remained topside. To an observer watching from above, the giant warship had been simply swallowed by the surging sea.

The descent below periscope depth brought them into a realm where their only sensory input was sound. The *Alabama* would now have to rely solely on its sonar to determine the presence of other vessels, both friendly and hostile.

"Captain," said the quartermaster from the adjoining navigation plot, "we're currently passing over the continental shelf and entering deep water."

Hunter watched as Ramsey crossed over to the navigation plotting station to have a closer look at the chart displayed there. Hunter decided to join him, and together they studied the progress of their current course, one that was taking them almost due west.

"Before we put the pedal to the metal, I want to make absolutely certain that we don't have one of those Akulas following in our baffles," said Ramsey, in reference to the sound-absorbent cone of water directly aft of the *Alabama*'s stern. "XO, I'd like you to spend some time in sonar while we begin our covert egress."

"Aye, aye, sir," replied Hunter, who listened as Ramsey issued a flurry of orders.

"COB, prepare to set up a detailed sonar search. Station the fire control tracking party. All ahead one-third. Rig the ship for ultra quiet."

This last order necessitated the shutdown of all machinery deemed not absolutely necessary for the ship's operation. The object was to make an already-quiet vessel even quieter. To help accomplish this state, those sailors not on duty were relegated to their bunks, where the possibility of making any unwanted noise was at a minimum.

"Quartermaster, verify the best depth for sonar search," continued Ramsey.

"Captain, best depth for sonar search is three-zero-zero feet."

"Very well. Helm, make your depth three-zero-zero feet," Ramsey ordered.

The planesman was in the process of pushing down on his steering yoke as Hunter headed out of the control room. The sonar compartment was located just forward of the helm, off the port passageway, and Hunter could feel the increased angle of their descent as the deck canted hard in the direction he was now traveling.

He entered the sonar room by way of a closed doorway. A hushed quiet prevailed in this dimly lit, equipment-packed compartment. Three large consoles dominated the room, with a trio of operators seated before their glowing CRT screens. All of these technicians wore headsets and were busy manipulating either a thin black joystick or addressing a square keyboard positioned beside their monitor screens.

"I've got a contact, Sup," said the sailor manning the broadband console. "Designate Sierra nine, biologic."

The current sonar supervisor, or Sup (pronounced "soup") for short, was a familiar-looking sailor. Hunter remembered briefly meeting him back at the pier. Chief sonarman Danny Rivetti emerged from the forward equipment space and acknowledged Hunter with a quick thumbs-up before personally checking the broadband monitor himself. Satisfied by what he saw there, Rivetti picked up the nearest intercom handset, which hung from the cable-lined ceiling.

"Conn, sonar," he reported, his heavy New York accent most obvious. "We have a new contact, bearing one-six-six. Designate Sierra nine, biologic."

"Sonar, conn, designate Sierra nine biologic. Aye, sonar," returned a voice from the overhead intercom speaker.

"Good work, babe," said Rivetti to the sailor responsible for monitoring the broadband console.

Rivetti placed the intercom handset in its cradle and turned to greet the newcomer in their midst. "Welcome to the 'Bama's sonar shack, sir."

Hunter nodded and found himself liking the senior sonarman right off. He displayed an easygoing, professional presence, and seemed most personable.

"Sir, would you like to have a seat at one of the consoles?" asked Rivetti.

"That's really not necessary, but thanks all the same," returned Hunter, who positioned himself behind the middle operator and surveyed each of the three stations.

The screens themselves displayed a compilation of data collected by a variety of sound monitors. The *Alabama*'s spherical sonar array occupied the boat's bow. This fifteen-foot-diameter sphere of ultrasensitive hydrophones was enhanced by a low-frequency, passive conformal array mounted throughout the hull. To provide medium range detection of low-frequency noises, their towed array was presently deployed. This passive system was stowed in a tubular shroud on the hull's port side, and was fed from a reel in the port horizontal stabilizer. The array's cable was over 2,500 feet long, and 3.5 inches thick, with the 240-foot-long hydrophone array positioned at the cable's very end.

Their next contact emanated from the waterfall display of the console responsible for monitoring the towed array. "Sup," said the technician manning this console, "it looks like we've got us a surface contact in our baffles. Bearing one-one-five, max range."

Both Rivetti and Hunter peered over the technician's shoulder to identify the contact. Having participated in his fair share of sonar watches, Hunter intently studied the green-tinted screen. The top of the display showed the bearing of their contact, while the vertical scale showed its frequency.

"What do you think, sir?" asked Rivetti casually.

Almost feeling like he was being put to the test, Hunter pointed to the thickest of the individual white lines forming the waterfall pattern. "At that range, that signal's coming in awfully strong to be a fishing trawler or pleasure boat. I'd say that we've tagged a merchant."

"My feeling exactly," replied Rivetti as he reached up for the intercom to report this new contact to the conn.

Hunter was pleasantly surprised when the senior sonar supervisor proceeded to remove a large bag of Hershey chocolate Kisses from an overhead ventilation duct. Like a mother hen feeding its chicks, he handed each of his men a handful of candies, making certain to include Hunter.

"I always take care of my men when they take care of me," added Rivetti, before biting into a candy.

Hunter unwrapped one of the cone-shaped chocolates and reflected. "It seems that Hershey Kisses are my daughter's very favorite food nowadays."

"Mine too," returned Rivetti. "How old's your kid?"

Hunter grinned. "Her fifth birthday was yesterday."

"You don't say. My little bit just turned two last week."

Rivetti proudly pulled a picture from his breast pocket and handed it to Hunter. It showed a smiling imp of a girl, with long, curly brown hair and big, dark, devilish eyes.

''This one's gonna be a real heartbreaker,'' Hunter observed.

Any further personal chatter was cut short by the voice of the broadband operator. ''I'm picking up some high-frequency biological noise due north of us, Sup.''

''Pipe it through the overhead, babe,'' Rivetti instructed while chewing on a chocolate.

Hunter listened as a series of unworldly sounds filled the compartment. They ranged from a shrill, drawn-out squeal to a deep, guttural bellow, and could only come from a single underwater species.

''Sounds like those whales are squawking away like a bunch of old women,'' observed Rivetti, who glanced at Hunter and confidentially added, ''Sir, it appears that all we're sharin' these seas with are a bunch of boisterous whales, some horny shrimp, and that merchant behind us. If you ask me, I'd say that the *'Bama*'s baffles are clear, and that means we're ready to rock 'n' roll!''

The sixth day of the USS *Alabama*'s patrol found the warship well out into the deep waters of the central Pacific. By then, the crew had collectively adjusted to a new time frame, in which the twenty-four-hour clock was no longer relevant. Their master was now the machine they sailed inside, and to best serve it, an eighteen-hour schedule was instituted. Six hours of duty were followed by a twelve-hour break, then another six-hour duty slot.

Because they had remained submerged since their initial dive, and hadn't even ascended to periscope depth, the terms day and night had no meaning. An artificial world was thus created, with the crew aware of the passage of outside time only from the nature of the meal being served.

Because of the confined, rote nature of their dangerous work, food was a very important element of a submariner's life. Mealtimes were looked at with great anticipation, not only to feed the body, but to provide nourishment for social appetites as well.

Chief Howard Rono was the current master of the *Alabama*'s galley. A Southerner by birth, the fit, crew-cut, thirty-three-year-old master chef was extremely proud of the chow that they served. The feeding of 150 men three meals a day and snacks was no easy task in itself. Space considerations limited the size of the galley and his staff. With many patrols lasting well over sixty days, having adequate foodstuffs available was a constant concern. Though the *Alabama*'s larder was more spacious than those previous classes of submarine that he had sailed upon, Rono was extra cautious when monitoring the crew's consumption.

Beyond the fear of actually running out of food, Rono planned his meals with care, always taking into account the crew's health. The relatively inactive life of a submariner could play havoc with the waistline, and a physically ill sailor would do them no good should an alert be received.

Chief Rono's current health passion was cutting down on the crew's consumption of red meat and fried foods. He was accomplishing this by serving lean turkey by-products whenever possible. And since the young sailors that he catered to weren't long out of high school, he satisfied their taste for fried foods by substituting low-cholesterol canola oil in their deep fat fryer.

This evening's meal was a prime example of how such a healthy menu could be adapted to suit the men's taste. Ground turkey burgers provided the main course, with corn, coleslaw, and onion rings on the side. Nonfat peach yogurt was being served for dessert, and Rono seriously doubted that any of his customers would even be aware of the meal's low fat content.

So far, he had yet to hear a single word of complaint. After making certain that his cooks had the majority of the actual food preparation completed, Rono slipped off into the crew's mess to subtly gauge their reactions.

He spotted the perfect place to begin this unofficial survey at the table just aft of the beverage dispensers. As usual, the COB was holding court there, with chiefs Marichek and Hunsicker his captive audience. Each of these individuals sported a bulging belly, at the very limit of naval regulations, and if the chow passed their muster, Rono was in.

"How's the vittles, gents?" he asked as he sauntered up to their table and sat down in a vacant chair.

The COB was just finishing up a joke about a traveling salesman and a dolphin, and while Rono patiently waited for him to finish, he inspected their plates. He allowed himself the barest of relieved grins upon finding them wiped clean, except for a few onion rings.

"Hey there, Cookie," said the COB after delivering his joke's tasteless punch line. "The burgers were excellent, though your rings left a little to be desired."

"What's wrong with 'em?" Rono worriedly asked.

COB displayed the finicky finesse of a lifelong junk food gourmand, as he picked up his fork and flaked off the golden brown coating of one of his uneaten onion rings. "Your fire's too hot, Cookie. This ring's near burnt to a crisp!"

Rono bent over to have a closer look at the COB's plate, and he took a close-up look at the suspect coating. "It does look a little brown," he admitted. "I knew that I should have replaced that deep fat fryer thermostat during our last refit.''

"Take it easy, Cookie," advised the COB. "It ain't the end of the world, and you're still the best friggin' cook in the fleet.''

"I'll second that," said Rick Marichek as he leaned back and contentedly patted his protruding beer belly. "Burnt rings or not, my previous offer still stands, Howard. When you're done with the navy, me and my LuAnn will have a job waiting for you at our resort.''

"So you're still goin' through with it, Ricky," said Rono.

"You'd better believe it," snapped Marichek. "As I was just tellin' COB and Hunsy here, LuAnn's father signed over the property title to us on the day before we left Bangor. That makes us the proud owners of seventy-five scenic, lakeside acres outside beautiful Eureka Springs, Arkansas.''

"I still want to know how you're gonna be able to afford developing this raw property into a proper resort," wondered Chief Hunsicker.

Marichek nonchalantly gestured. "No problem, Hunsy. As soon as me and the U.S. Navy part ways at the end of this patrol, I'm gonna have all the time that I need to clear the land and lay those trailer pads. Don't forget that LuAnn's pappy is a master carpenter, and he promised to help me construct the main lodge once the trailer park's ready.''

"Sounds like a plan," said the COB.

Any further discussion on their part was abruptly made impossible by an excited chorus of shouts coming from a group of sailors seated at an adjoining table. The men there had their glances glued to the overhead video monitor, where a pre-recorded football game was being shown. Rono recognized the action as belonging to the final nail-biting moments of last year's Army-Navy game. Shrugging his shoulders, he lightly commented. "That's gotta be the third time this patrol that they watched that same damn game."

"I'll say," concurred the COB. "And no matter how many times they see that rerun, Navy's still gonna lose!"

Directly forward of the crew's mess, on the other side of the shared galley, was the *Alabama*'s wardroom. Except for a single enlisted mess attendant, this was a segregated realm—the exclusive dining area of the ship's officers.

Though all of the crew shared the same menu, it was the wardroom's formal decorum that somehow made the food taste a bit different there. The room itself exuded a warm ambience, its simulated wood-grain walls promoting a men's club atmosphere. The spacious central table, which could be converted into an operating theater should conditions demand, was always covered with a dark blue tablecloth. The china and silverware were practical and sturdy, each piece decorated with the boat's emblem.

Instead of the freewheeling cafeteria-style service of the crew's mess, the dining here had a definite ritualized format. It all started with the captain's arrival at his customary place at the head of the table. The XO's seat was to his right, with Chop's place on the far end of the table, directly opposite the captain. The rest of the dining positions were generally unassigned and available on a first-come basis.

Unless otherwise directed, it was Frank Ramsey who was responsible for selecting the evening's music. The wardroom offered a varied selection of CDs, ranging from country to rock, from new age to classical. Ramsey's taste tended toward the latter, and this evening's selection was one of his very favorites. As he was so fond of reminding his men, Tchaikovsky's Sixth Symphony, *Pathétique*, was in his opinion one of the most expressive pieces of music ever composed.

As the symphony's soulful Adagio filled the wardroom, the meal got under way with the arrival of their salads. This evening, the first course was comprised of coleslaw, which arrived in a communal silver tureen and was first offered to the captain. Ramsey helped himself to a portion, then passed the tureen to Hunter, who subsequently handed it to the officer seated to his right, in this case, Darik Westerguard. The rest of their meal was served in a similar manner, and by the time their turkey burgers, corn, and onion rings were consumed, and the yogurt and coffee arrived, only five of the ship's officers remained at the table.

With Bear curled up beneath Ramsey's chair, having eaten his fair share of table scraps, the conversation gradually shifted from small talk to much more serious matters. No doubt influenced by tonight's musical selection, their current topic began with a discussion of Russian composers. It all too soon shifted to a spirited debate revolving around Russia's present political crisis and the man most responsible for it—Vladimir Radchenko.

"I still don't get it," admitted a very perplexed Roy Zimmer, who was seated to the right of Chop and directly across from Darik Westerguard. "The man's a fanatic, pure and simple. In my opinion, he's just another Hitler. Why doesn't somebody just kill him?"

"Good idea," said Chop while pouring himself another cup of coffee.

"Don't forget that it's fanatics that make history," reminded Darik Westerguard. "Patton was a fanatic. That's what made him great."

Zimmer would have no part of this line of reasoning, and he expressed himself accordingly. "I guess Radchenko's not just a fanatic, but a dangerous lunatic as well, that's threatening to start a nuclear war."

"So what does that make us?" interrupted Weps from his position on Zimmer's right. "Don't forget, we're the only nation to ever actually drop a nuclear bomb."

With this statement, Ramsey briefly caught Hunter's glance. Hunter could tell that his CO was enjoying this debate, and he was beginning to wonder why Ramsey was not actively participating in it.

"There's a half dozen other third world countries with nuclear bombs who'd love to drop one on us," offered Westerguard.

"Well, we're just gonna have to drop one on them first," jested Chop.

Zimmer disgustedly shook his head. "Shut up, Dougherty."

"Why don't you both shut up?" blurted Weps.

Realizing that it was time to intervene, Ramsey

coolly quizzed his XO. "Do you think it was a mistake, Mr. Hunter?"

"Sir?" questioned Hunter, not really sure what he was referring to.

"Using the bomb on Hiroshima and Nagasaki," Ramsey clarified.

Hunter pushed aside his half-filled coffee cup and thought a moment before replying. "Well, sir, if I thought that it was a mistake, I wouldn't be here, would I?"

Ramsey grunted. "That's very interesting, the way that you put that."

"Oh, and how did I put it, sir?" snapped Hunter.

"Very carefully," responded Ramsey.

A certain tenseness accompanied this exchange, and the *Alabama*'s junior officers breathlessly watched as their outspoken commanding officer continued.

"Mr. Hunter, you do have a certain way of qualifying your remarks. If somebody asked me whether we should've used the bomb on Japan, it's a simple yes on my part. By all means, I'd say. Drop the fucker, twice if necessary."

Hunter appeared to be flustered by the captain's blunt observation, and Ramsey quickly interceded to vent his XO's unease.

"Please don't get me wrong, Mr. Hunter. I'm not suggesting that you're indecisive. Not at all. You're just complicated. But that's the way the navy wanted you. Me, they wanted simple."

"Well, sir," offered Hunter, "you sure fooled them."

Ramsey stifled a laugh. "Be careful, Mr. Hunter. Being a simpleminded son of a bitch is all I've got to rely on. Hyman Rickover personally gave me my first command with a checklist, a target, and a button to push. All I had to know was how to push it, and they'd tell me when. But it appears that the post-Rickover navy wants you to know why.''

Hunter seemed confused. ''Don't they want us all to know why, sir?''

Ramsey sat back in his chair and thoughtfully answered. ''In the Naval War College, it was metallurgy, electrical engineering, and nuclear physics, not nineteenth century philosophies such as von Clauswitz's 'war is a continuation of national policy by other means.' ''

Hunter was quick to pick up on this line of reasoning. ''I think what von Clauswitz was trying to say was a little more . . .''

''Complicated?'' offered Ramsey.

Hunter shook his head and continued on with the quote that Ramsey had brought up. '' 'That while the purpose of war is to serve a political end, the nature of war is to serve itself.' ''

Ramsey scanned the rapt faces of his fellow officers before returning his gaze to his XO. ''I'm impressed, Mr. Hunter. In other words, the sailor most likely to win the war is the one most willing to part company with politicians and ignore everything but the destruction of the enemy. Would you agree?''

''I agree that's what he meant,'' Hunter said hesitantly.

''But you don't agree with him?'' persisted Ramsey.

''No, sir, not in a nuclear war,'' Hunter managed. "I don't believe the real enemy can be destroyed."

"Oh, is that so?" said Ramsey, while carefully rolling up his cloth napkin and sliding it into an engraved silver napkin ring. "Please tell us, Mr. Hunter. Exactly who is the real enemy?"

Well aware that all eyes were upon him, Hunter replied as honestly as possible. "In a nuclear war, sir, I believe that the real enemy is war itself!"

7

Hunter had little interaction with Ramsey in the days immediately following their intense wardroom exchange. This wasn't on purpose, but the result of scheduling differences. For the most part, Hunter's watches took place while the captain was off duty, with the converse true when Ramsey had the watch. Meals were no exception, and the boat's two senior officers seldom had a chance to share dining times.

By the time the second week of their patrol was coming to an end, Hunter was completely adjusted to life inside the USS *Alabama*. He had learned most of his new shipmates' names and, more importantly, had gotten a better understanding of their individual strengths and weaknesses. He had also managed to make a major dent in his paperwork, and he soon hoped to be able to see the surface of his desk once again.

To assist in his adjustment to the undersea life, he made certain to establish a strict exercise routine. It was a habit that he had initiated during his first submarine patrol, almost two decades earlier. The vessel that he had been assigned to at that time was an attack boat, its tight confines in stark contrast to the rather spacious environs of the *Alabama*. And though running was out of the question, they did have a couple of stationary bicycles and rowing machines stashed away in the reactor spaces.

Hunter's very favorite exercise, though, was running, and only when he was assigned to his first boomer did he learn to make the best use of the boat's missile compartment for this endeavor. He tried his best to run each and every day, and the current patrol was no exception.

Hunter was presently well into his daily jog. His gray *Alabama* sweats were already stained with perspiration, and he did his best to lengthen his stride, all the while avoiding the protruding cables and electrical boxes that made exercising here a real challenge.

He found the best place to run to be the upper level of the missile compartment. Most often, there were a minimum number of crew members there, and thus fewer obstacles to be concerned with.

Other than the engineering spaces, which occupied the after end of the *Alabama*, the missile magazine was the largest single compartment on the boat. The launch canisters holding their twenty-four Trident missiles were positioned twelve to a side. The canisters themselves were painted an orangish red, with a light beige linoleum floor encircling them.

After walking the racetrack-shaped route with a pedometer, he was able to determine that nineteen laps constituted a mile. Though the running of a marathon put one's knees and elbows in constant peril, the few bumps and bruises he suffered were well worth the risk.

To get the best workout of his cardiovascular system, he paced himself with his digital watch. His first mile of the day had taken him six minutes and eleven seconds to complete, and he hoped to break the six-minute threshold during the mile he was presently in the midst of.

With the heels of his nylon running shoes monotonously slapping against the highly polished linoleum tiling, he rounded the forward end of the compartment beyond which the navigation station and control room were situated, and headed amidships, back toward the engine room. The missiles themselves could be accessed from three separate levels, and it was on this upper one that the warheads were serviced.

Only a handful of sailors were at work here this afternoon, their efforts focused on replacing a pressure release valve on tube number five. As Hunter sprinted past the work party, he spotted the only other visible crew member standing in the center of the compartment between tubes number eleven and twelve. This dungaree-clad, blond-haired seaman had originally arrived in the missile room just as Hunter was completing his first mile. His unique duty lay at the other end of the stout leash that he had securely wrapped around his wrist. It seemed that Bear also enjoyed stretching his legs on a daily basis, and the young sailor's responsibility was to escort the ship's mascot wherever he cared to go. Hunter couldn't miss the sailor's perplexed expression, and the fact that the pooper-scooper that he held in his free hand was still empty.

Hunter briefly shortened his stride while preparing to round the after end of the compartment, and his thoughts shifted to the terrier's enigmatic master. The mere idea of a submarine captain bringing his pet dog along on a patrol was surely without precedent. Hunter had never heard of such a thing before, and he wondered how Command could allow such an obvious breach of regulations. They surely knew of Bear's presence aboard the *Alabama*, and by tolerating the dog, they were giving their blessings to yet another of Ramsey's unique idiosyncrasies.

Hunter increased his stride as he began his way down the port passageway. It was apparent that there were many areas where Ramsey's ideas about life in general were the exact opposite of his own. Though they might not always be in agreement in such matters as politics and ethics, this didn't lessen Hunter's sincere respect for the man professionally. His natural leadership abilities couldn't be ignored. The crew virtually worshiped the man, and even Hunter felt a bit more secure knowing that a veteran like Ramsey was there should things get ugly.

Hunter supposed that their basic differences were the result of vastly contrasting upbringings. Beyond the obvious racial differences, Ramsey was the by-product of another era. His political beliefs were forged during the heyday of Soviet-American confrontation, making him the consummate cold warrior. At forty-nine, Ramsey was one of the oldest active submarine captains in the fleet, and Hunter knew that there was much that he could learn from such a veteran. Because a new crop of talented, younger officers were anxiously waiting in the ranks for those ever-decreasing command spots, Ramsey's days of active service were on the wane. In fact, this patrol could very well be Ramsey's last, and Hunter would do his best to take advantage of the hand fate had dealt him.

The soft beeping from his digital watch distracted Hunter. He double-checked the time and knew that if he was going to break that six-minute mile, he'd have to turn on the afterburners.

He whizzed past the work party and did his best to fully extend his legs and pump his arms. Ignoring the sweat that thoroughly soaked his brow, he concentrated his efforts solely on regulating his heaving breath. This was a trick that his wife had first taught him.

Julia had been a track star in high school and college. Her specialty was the 440, though her real love was the marathon.

She first taught him the vital importance of regulating one's breath while running during a jog to Mount Vernon on the Alexandria, Virginia, bike trail. That was during the early days of their marriage, when Hunter was temporarily assigned to the Pentagon.

His eventual mastering of this difficult technique did much to improve both his speed and stamina. Their frequent jaunts to Mount Vernon became even more enjoyable as Hunter was able to better keep up with his wife, and all the while enjoy the passing scenery.

By the time he rounded the after end of the missile compartment and began his way down the straight passageway that lay ahead of him, he was satisfied that his pace was just sufficient to attain his goal. His rhythmic breaths were deep and constant, and he briefly lowered his arms to shake them vigorously and loosen the cramped muscles in his shoulders.

An endorphin high possessed him as he sprinted by Bear and saw that his attendant was finally putting the pooper-scooper to work. Fighting the sudden urge to laugh out loud, Hunter was abruptly called back to reality by a sobering announcement over the public address system.

"Fire in the galley! Fire in the galley!"

The steady bonging of the fire alarm emphasized this alert, and Hunter let his instincts take over. Without a moment's hesitation, he sprinted for the aft accessway and quickly negotiated its steep ladder downward. Fire was one of the most terrifying disasters that could occur on a submarine, for if the flames didn't kill you, the toxic fumes and smoke would.

His actions guided by hundreds of previous drills, Hunter's immediate destination was the fire scene. The alarm was still madly bonging away in the background as he climbed down the final ladder and dropped onto the deck at the aft end of the vessel's third level. This lower portion of the missile compartment was where the crew's berths were located, and as he turned forward to reach the galley, he was faced with a crowded passageway rapidly filling with enlisted men on their way to their individual fire stations.

The majority of these sailors already had their EABs in hand. Short for Emergency Air Breather, this rubber mask sported a clear plastic viewing port. Once on station, the EAB's breathing tube would be connected to an overhead manifold, where fresh air would be available to be pumped into the mask with the assistance of a regulator.

As Hunter pushed his way past the slowest-moving enlisted men, thick black smoke began pouring out of the forward hatch. The sudden realization that this wasn't a drill after all barely had time to register in his mind, as he plowed through the circular hatch feetfirst. This put him in a passageway directly adjoining the crew's mess. The smoke was incredibly thick there, and after ordering the hatch sealed behind him, Hunter headed for the galley's scullery. It was there, above the main washbasin, that he found his own EAB, stowed in a small locker.

Though his eyes stung and his breathing was labored, he was able to pull the mask over his head and tighten its restraining straps. This particular EAB was a portable unit, with its own carbon dioxide scrubber enclosed, and Hunter continued on to the galley, confident that he'd have at least thirty minutes of breathable air.

A swinging doorway led into the galley. Billowing clouds of thick black smoke forced Hunter to a temporary halt, and it was here he encountered Chief Rono. The vessel's head cook also wore a portable EAB, and from the blackened smudges that completely stained his apron, it was obvious that he had just emerged from the fire scene.

Rono appeared to be close to panicking as he beckoned Hunter to join him back beside the scullery. By the time they initiated this brief retreat, the first members of the fire team arrived. They, too, were outfitted with portable EABs, and had asbestos flash suppressors protecting their eyes. As they readied their hose, which had a long, tapered metal nozzle on its end, Chief Rono desperately addressed Hunter.

"Sir, the fire started in the deep fat fryer. Chief Marichek's still in there, tryin' to activate the range guard extinguisher!"

Hunter readily took control of the situation. His first duty was to inform the control room of their predicament.

"This is the XO," he barked into the nearest intercom handset. "I'm in charge in the crew's mess. Pressurize the third level fire hose!"

"Come on!" he shouted to the members of the fire team after hanging up the handset. "I'll take the nozzle position. Let's work some more of that hose in here!"

Hunter quickly fitted a flash suppressor over his mask, and after putting on a pair of fire-resistant gloves, he tightly gripped the hose's nozzle and charged into the galley. The roiling smoke all but blinded him, but he continued moving forward regardless, prompted by the terrifying sight of flames flickering nearby. The fire indeed appeared to be coming from the direction of the deep fat fryer, and he wasted no time flicking open the nozzle's release valve. A powerful white stream of fire-retardant foam shot out, and Hunter tried his best to smother the flames.

Oblivious to any possible danger to himself, he moved in to attack the conflagration head-on. At the moment, only one thing mattered to Hunter, and that was to extinguish the flames as selflessly and efficiently as one killed an enemy on a battle-field.

As the foam continued to spew from the nozzle, Hunter was suddenly aware of the stifling heat. He found it difficult to breathe, and, for a confusing second, a wave of dizziness overcame him. Yet the spell passed, and Hunter became aware of other members of the fire-fighting team at his side, with their own hoses pumping out foam.

One member of the team held a compact, battery-powered, infrared tracking device up to his brow. In such a manner he was able to see through the billowing smoke and determine the presence of any hot spots that might have escaped them.

"The fire appears to be out!" he observed after thoroughly scanning the scene.

With this report, Hunter's concerns shifted from extinguishing the fire to locating their missing shipmate. "Where the hell's Chief Marichek?" he questioned.

Hunter dropped the nozzle and impatiently grabbed the infrared scanning device. With its viewing lens up to his eyes, the smoke-filled room miraculously cleared. The area where the deep fat fryer was located was buried in white foam, and as he looked at the base of the fryer he spotted the sole of a large shoe protruding from the foam. Hunter immediately rushed forward and found the portly master chief curled up on the floor, with his EAB pulled tightly over his head. He didn't appear to be conscious, and Hunter needed the assistance of two brawny members of the fire party to carry Marichek out into the crew's mess.

The smoke had sufficiently cleared in that portion of the ship so Hunter was able to remove his EAB, and Marichek's as well. The sub's corpsman arrived on the scene and quickly determined the incapacitated chief's vital signs.

"He's still alive," reported the corpsman, after checking Marichek's pulse. "The big guy's probably suffering from smoke inhalation. I'll hit him with some oxygen and we'll take it from there."

Hunter watched as the corpsman fitted an oxygen mask over Marichek's plump face and only then remembered that he owed the control room a call. The nearest intercom handset was positioned beside the scullery, and as he crossed the mess to remove the handset from its cradle, a loud spasm of coughing exploded behind him. Marichek, a quick glance revealed, would be OK. Relieved to have the veteran back among the living, Hunter took up the handset.

"This is the XO. The fire is out. Reflash watch is stationed in the galley. The damages appear to be confined to the deep fat fryer, with no serious injuries, except for a suspected case of smoke inhalation."

Inside the *Alabama*'s control room, Hunter's report was received with a shared sense of relief. Frank Ramsey was particularly delighted to hear the news, for it put an end to the great dilemma he had just been facing.

Not really knowing if the fire would be controlled or not, he was being forced to pick from a rapidly dwindling number of options. The most prudent course of action would have been to surface immediately. Once topside, they'd be able to vent the smoke more effectively and concentrate their efforts on containing the blaze.

What caused Ramsey to hesitate ordering this ascent was the very nature of their current mission. The USS *Alabama* derived its effectiveness as a deterrent by remaining submerged at all costs. A trip to the surface could have disastrous implications, opening them up to unwanted detection. This was especially relevant now that they were operating under an alert status of DEFCON Four. Thus Ramsey hoped to keep his warship hidden beneath the Pacific as long as humanly possible. By the grace of God, his men had come through, and, because of their superb training, the fire had been extinguished and the *Alabama*'s covertness subsequently ensured.

"Sir," said the quartermaster as he joined Ramsey on the control room's periscope pedestal, "damage control reports that the smoke has cleared from the galley. The atmosphere has returned to normal."

Ramsey yanked off his EAB. As he pulled out the oxygen hose from the overhead manifold, there was a brief snap of compressed air.

"All hands, remove EABs" he instructed the quartermaster.

This order was relayed via the 1MC, and, throughout the ship, the dreaded emergency process known as "sucking rubber" was mercifully terminated. The control room crew was most happy to have the crisis behind them, and Ramsey listened as a wave of relieved chatter escaped their lips. There appeared to be a naive innocence to this hushed celebration that bothered Ramsey, and he decided it was time to push them one step farther and see how tough they really were.

Ramsey excused himself for the adjoining radio room. He found Lieutenant Zimmer there, in the process of stowing away his EAB. Petty Officer Russell Vossler was in the forwardmost portion of the equipment-clogged compartment unpacking a box of computer paper, and Ramsey deliberately whispered into Zimmer's ear so that Vossler wouldn't hear him.

Ramsey's confidential message was brief, and Zimmer gave his captain just enough time to slip into the shadows of the nearby OPCON before turning to address his computer keyboard. Seconds later, a muted electronic alarm filled the radio room with undulating sound. Russell Vossler responded to this alarm by hurrying over to the main communications console, where a quarter-sized red button marked *EAM* began blinking. It was while Vossler scanned his monitor screen that Ramsey pulled a stopwatch from his pocket. Ramsey started its timer and then calmly returned to the control room.

He arrived back on the periscope pedestal just as Petty Officer Vossler's excited voice emanated from the overhead speaker.

"Conn, radio, we are receiving flash traffic!"

Ramsey watched as Lieutenant Westerguard, their current OOD, reacted to this. "Radio, conn, aye," he responded via the intercom.

Vossler's next report was only seconds in coming. "Conn, radio, the flash traffic is, exercise Emergency Action Message, for weapons system readiness test."

"Radio, conn, aye," the OOD replied before addressing the entire crew on the IMC. "Alert One! Alert One! Man battle stations missile for weapons system readiness test!"

This unexpected call to battle stations caught Hunter peering behind the still-smoking remains of the deep fat fryer, with Chief Rono close at his side. With the steady sound of the general alarm bonging away in the background, Hunter disgustedly broke off his inspection and turned to address his equally surprised shipmate.

"Do you believe it, Chief? A fucking missile drill, now of all times!"

Knowing full well that his proper place for the drill was in the control room, Hunter added, "Chief, you're in charge down here. Have your men pull those bulkhead panels. And if there's the least hint of a flare-up, notify me in the conn at once!"

The next stage of the weapons system readiness test took Ramsey back into the OPCON. This cramped compartment directly adjoined the radio room. Its main feature was a small three-person booth, and a console topped with a trio of locked steel safes labeled TOP SECRET.

The nerve-racking bonging of the general alarm finally ran its course, and both lieutenants Zimmer and Westerguard joined their captain. Together they held the telegram-sized Emergency Action Message (EAM), that Petty Officer Vossler had previously torn off the radio console's printer.

"Sir," said Zimmer. "We have a properly formatted Emergency Action Message for weapons system readiness test."

"I concur, sir," snapped Westerguard.

"Request permission to remove the authenticator, sir," Zimmer added.

Ramsey anxiously peered down at his ticking stopwatch and angrily retorted. "You know I can't allow you to authenticate without the presence of the XO. Where the hell is he, anyway?"

No sooner were those words spoken than Hunter breathlessly ducked into the OPCON. Not interested in excuses, Ramsey shook his head.

"How good of you to make it, Mr. Hunter. Lieutenant Zimmer, get that authenticator!"

Now that the XO had arrived, both Zimmer and Westerguard were allowed to approach the largest of the OPCON's three safes. It was Zimmer who first addressed the tumbler and opened the outer door. Another locked door lay inside, and this time it was Westerguard who dialed in the proper combination and opened it.

Both men then reached into the inner safe and pulled out the sealed authenticator packet and a dummy, wooden captain's missile indicator panel key. They held the items in both their hands and turned for the booth.

"Request permission to authenticate, sir," asked Zimmer.

"Permission granted," Ramsey answered. "Authenticate."

Both junior officers proceeded to tear open the plastic packet and pull out the laminated authenticator card. They placed this card on the table, and began matching its contents with the dummy EAM.

"Alpha. Alpha. Bravo. Echo. Charlie. Zulu. Tango," said Zimmer.

Westerguard repeated this exact same sequence, prompting Zimmer to look up and directly address Ramsey. "Message is authentic, sir."

"I concur, sir," added Westerguard.

Hunter quickly double-checked their work. "I agree, Captain."

"Sir, here is your captain's missile key," said Zimmer as he handed over the dummy key.

Ramsey attached this key to a lanyard that he wore around his neck and solemnly spoke to his XO. "Mr. Hunter, would you please join me at the missile indicator launch panel?"

The launch panel was positioned immediately aft of the diving control station in the adjoining control room. Displayed on its compact length were a multiple series of buttons marked 1SQ, DENOTE, PREPARE, and AWAY. The series referred to the operational status of each of their Trident missiles, and was repeated in a horizontal line twenty-four times. At the bottom of the panel was a single lock, and it was there that the captain's missile key would be inserted and turned to permit missile launch.

With all the seriousness of an actual launch, Ramsey positioned himself behind this panel. Hunter stood on his left and listened as Ramsey addressed the entire crew over the 1MC.

"Set condition 1SQ for weapons system readiness test. This is the captain. This is an exercise."

Strategic missile launch protocol demanded that the vessel's XO repeat this order to the crew, and Hunter readily complied. "Set condition 1SQ for weapons system readiness test. This is the XO. This is an exercise."

Hunter hung up the intercom handset and looked to his right and discreetly whispered to Ramsey. "Sir, that fire in the galley could still flare up."

Ramsey wanted no part of such information and angrily retorted, "For God's sake, Mr. Hunter. We're in the middle of a weapons system readiness drill, and now is not the time!"

Quick to regain his composure with a deep breath, Ramsey directed his next remarks to the COB, who was their current diving officer. "COB, make your depth one-five-zero feet, and prepare to hover."

"One-five-zero feet, aye, sir," the COB repeated.

While the helmsmen carried out the depth change, Ramsey readdressed the intercom. "Weapons, conn, this is the captain. Simulate pressurizing all missile tubes."

Per protocol, Hunter repeated this order. "Weapons, conn, this is the XO. Simulate pressurizing all missile tubes."

"Conn, weapons," broke a voice over the overhead speaker. "Simulate pressurizing all missile tubes, aye, sir."

The captain's missile indicator panel suddenly lit up. The twenty-four buttons marked 1SQ were conspicuously red, and would only turn green when the launch and targeting systems of each individual Trident were warmed up and ready for firing.

Ramsey impatiently looked at his stopwatch before picking up the intercom. "Weapons, this is the captain. Request approximate time to weapons system 1SQ."

"Captain, weapons, approximate time to weapons system 1SQ is fourteen minutes, sir,'' broke a voice over the public address system.

"Ship is at launch depth and ready to hover, Captain," informed the COB from the helm.

"Very well, COB. Commence hovering," Ramsey instructed.

"Commence hovering, aye, sir."

Unable to miss the stopwatch that Ramsey kept peeking at, Hunter reached for the notebook holding the launch procedures sequence checklist. As he began marking the plastic pages of this manual with a black felt-tip pen, another call arrived in the control room via its overhead speakers. The voice was not their weapons officer's, but that of Chief Howard Rono.

"Control, enlisted men's mess, Chief Marichek is undergoing cardiac arrest! We are beginning emergency CPR."

Ramsey first reacted to the disturbing news by clicking off his stopwatch. Only then did he address the crew over the 1MC.

"Gentlemen, this is the captain. May I have your attention? We have just received word that one of our shipmates is experiencing a medical problem, so we are terminating the drill. Secure from battle stations missile."

"Mr. Zimmer, take the conn," Ramsey added to the new OOD. "I'll be below with the XO."

It was Hunter who led the way down to the sub's third level. They entered the crew's mess and found a half dozen sailors gathered at the center of the compartment. Their attention was riveted on the efforts of two of their shipmates, who were desperately working on the prone, unmoving body of Chief Marichek. Both Hunter and Ramsey pushed their way past the gawkers and watched while Chief Rono administered mouth-to-mouth, and their corpsman, CPR.

"Come on, big guy," Rono urged between breaths. "Don't leave us, Ricky!"

The corpsman noted the arrival of the two senior officers and spoke to them while continuing his efforts. "It appears to have been a massive heart attack. One minute he was sitting up sipping some Joe, and next, he was reaching for his chest and gasping for air."

"Damn it, Ricky!" exclaimed the frustrated head cook. "For the sake of LuAnn and that new resort of yours, come back to us!"

After a futile search for any sort of pulse, the corpsman reluctantly stopped pumping on Marichek's chest. He looked at Rono and sadly shook his head.

"It's useless, Chief," he whispered. "He's gone."

Only then did the finality of the moment sink in, and Rono immediately blamed himself for this tragedy. "It's all my fault. If I had replaced that deep fat fryer thermostat, none of this would've happened."

"Nonsense," Ramsey uttered. "This is no time to feel sorry for yourself, Chief. All of us are saddened by this unfortunate loss, but our mission goes on. We're gonna need to seal the corpse in a body bag and stow it in the deep freeze. Then all of you are gonna have to get your keisters in gear and clean up this galley."

"Mr. Hunter," he added, "you I'd like to see in my stateroom."

Hunter was little prepared for the passionate exchange that soon followed as he made his way up to the second level and entered the captain's stateroom. Without bothering to offer his guest a chair, Ramsey sat down behind his desk. Bear climbed into his lap, and Ramsey began his diatribe while idly stroking his contented pet.

"So, Mr. Hunter, do you feel that I was in the wrong for running that drill?"

Hunter briefly hesitated. "Not necessarily, sir."

"Do you believe that I got that man killed?" Ramsey continued.

"No, sir. One thing had nothing to do with the other. This was an accident."

Not buying the sincerity of the XO's response, Ramsey altered tacks. "Would you have run the drill?"

"No, sir. I would not."

"And why not?"

"Well, sir, the fire in the galley could have flared back up. I'd have taken care of it first."

Ramsey sardonically grinned. "I'm sure you would have. Me, on the other hand, I tend to think that's the best time to have a drill. Confusion on a ship is nothing to fear; it should be taken advantage of. Lest you forget, Mr. Hunter, we are a ship of war, designed for battle. You don't just fight battles when everything is hunky-dory.

"What did you think, son?" he asked after a short pause. "That I was just some crazy old coot putting everybody in harm's way just for the thrill of the moment?"

"That wasn't my first thought, sir," Hunter truthfully admitted. "No, sir, I did not think that. At the time, I was in the galley fighting the fire, and just didn't agree with your call."

This was the essence of the subject that Ramsey wanted to explore and he softened his approach by offering Hunter a seat opposite him. The XO took the chair, and Ramsey continued.

"Just so we understand one another, Mr. Hunter. I have no problems with doubts or questions. As I told you before, I'm not seeking the company of kiss-asses. But when you've got something to say to me, you say it in private. And if privacy doesn't permit itself, you bite your fucking tongue. Because when we're at the conn, you and I are one! Are we clear about that, Commander?"

"Yes, sir," muttered Hunter softly.

"Those sailors out there are just boys," said Ramsey, trying hard to get his point across. "They're boys we are training to do a terrible unthinkable thing. And if the unthinkable ever occurs, the only reassurance they will have that they are doing the proper thing will derive from their unqualified belief in the unified chain of command. That means we do not question each other's actions in front of the crew! It means that we do not undermine each other! It means in a missile drill, that they hear your voice after mine, without hesitation! Do you agree with that policy, sailor?"

"Yes, sir, I do," Hunter softly replied.

Ramsey appeared to be in another world, his vacant stare angled off into space, his hand absentmindedly stroking Bear's neck.

"We are here to preserve democracy, Mr. Hunter, not to practice it."

With that declaration his concerns returned to more mundane matters. "There will be a memorial service for Chief Marichek in the enlisted men's mess at eleven hundred. Go see to it."

"Aye, sir," said Hunter, as he pushed back his chair to stand.

"Oh, and Hunter," Ramsey said as an afterthought. "I would like you to talk to the COB about his weight. I find it difficult, as I've known him for so long."

"Aye, sir."

Hunter stood and turned to leave the stateroom. Just as he grasped the doorknob, Ramsey's voice stopped him.

"Short of the outbreak of World War III, the ship sinking, or being attacked by a giant squid, I'd like to be undisturbed for the next thirty minutes."

"I'll see to it, sir," Hunter replied, suddenly aware of a strained, weary quality to the captain's voice.

"By the way, Mr. Hunter. It was Marichek's three hundred pounds that killed him, not the fire. Dismissed."

Hunter left Ramsey's quarters feeling emotionally drained. Unable to put his finger on what it was about their exchange that disturbed him so, he ducked into his own stateroom.

He couldn't sit down, and he found himself pacing to and fro like an animal in a cramped cage. The traumatic events of the past hour finally caught up with him, and he realized that he was still dressed in his sweats. His interrupted marathon seemed to have taken place a virtual lifetime ago. The fire, the missile drill, Marichek's death—all of those events had been compressed into a tight time frame. Capping all of it off was his one-on-one with Ramsey.

Hell, there was no way he felt the missile drill was in order. The fire had only just been snuffed out, and as far as they knew, a reflash could have popped up at any time. Since that was the case, why hadn't he stood his ground and been more forceful voicing his opinion to the captain? That was the reason for Hunter's being upset, and he smacked the palm of his hand against his desk to castigate himself for his inner weakness.

As the sound of the blow reverberated through the stateroom, Hunter caught sight of the framed picture of Julia gracing the desk. Viewing his beloved brought his composure back and he laughed at himself upon realizing how foolish his behavior was.

His moment of peace was but a short one. A vision of Marichek's pale, unmoving corpse possessed him, followed by an image of Frank Ramsey sanctimoniously petting his dog as he did his best to justify his rash decision to call the missile drill.

Though Hunter had certainly disagreed with his COs before, the discord between himself and Ramsey had somehow progressed to a personal level. For the first time, Hunter felt the stirrings of a genuine dislike for the man.

To properly work out his frustrations, he decided that a trip to the ship's punching bag was definitely in order. Still dressed in his sweats, he left his quarters, climbed down to the third level, and headed aft.

He passed by the galley and saw that Chief Rono and his men were already busy cleaning up the aftereffects of the fire. There were still 149 mouths to feed, though Hunter seriously doubted there'd be any more fried food during this patrol.

His transit took him into the missile compartment and past the crew's berthing spaces. Their living quarters were positioned between the tubes themselves. There were fourteen separate berths in all, with nine bunk bed–style cots apiece. At the aft end of the compartment, beside the ship's laundry, an Everlast punching bag was slung from the ceiling. Hunter had been an amateur boxer while at the Academy. Though his boxing career had been short, he did learn how to defend himself, and he knew of no better exercise to release one's tensions than pounding the ole punching bag.

Hunter recruited a passing sailor to hold the bag for him. With this curious seaman looking on, Hunter proceeded to attack the bag, first with a series of light jabs, and then with a furious flurry of body punches and uppercuts.

Ten minutes later he had had enough. His mind blessedly clear, he returned to his stateroom for a welcomed shower. The hot water on his aching shoulders was pure bliss, and after thoroughly scrubbing down his body, he squeegeed dry the stall's stainless steel walls and then slipped into a clean poopy suit.

Before returning to the galley to take a closer look at the fire damage and organize Marichek's memorial service, Hunter decided to stop off at the wardroom for some badly needed coffee. Since the next meal wasn't scheduled to be served for another hour yet, he was somewhat surprised to find Weps seated at the wardroom table. Peter Ince's wire rims were placed to the side of his partially filled ceramic mug, and his attention was focused on a slim paperback bound in blue. The mere fact that they were the only two black officers aboard the *Alabama* gave them a special bond.

"Whatcha reading?" Hunter casually asked.

Weps lowered the book and stretched his limbs. "It's titled *Submarine Detection From Space*, and if some of the stuff it says about Russian space-based laser capabilities is true, we could be in a shitload of trouble one day."

Hunter failed to follow this remark up, and Weps instinctively sensed that something was bothering him. "You okay, Ron?"

Hunter's frustrations exploded. "Does it make any sense to you to initiate a missile drill in the middle of a fire?"

"But the fire was out," snapped Weps, conscious now of what the something bothering Hunter was.

"And a man died," countered Hunter.

"Come on, Ron. That wasn't because of what the captain did."

Unable to exorcise his doubts, Hunter persisted. "A fire is a serious threat to the ship! Was he there? Did he even bother checking it out?"

"Look," said Weps using his most diplomatic manner, "you want to get along with the skipper, you gotta understand the guy. To him, you're Annapolis, Harvard, an expert on theory, and the consummate overachiever. Ramsey's had his head up his ass drivin' submarines for twenty-five years. Maybe he feels a little paranoid or inferior about the new, well-educated black kid on the block. If you ask me, the horse conversation was a perfect example of an effort to impress you."

"And that he did," Hunter revealed.

Weps watched as Hunter poured himself a cup of coffee and decided that a sympathetic approach was the proper one. "Why don't you lighten up on the guy, Ron? Look, his wife dumped him because of the navy. So submarines and that little dog of his are all he's got. And now that he's coming to the end of his active career, it's only natural that he's gonna be a bit touchy."

"So?" asked Hunter, his face finally relaxing in a smile.

Seeing this, Weps sarcastically underscored his response with his pointed right index finger. "So watch out, my friend. Because you'd better not ever forget that the skipper's favorite occupation of late is nailing his XOs!"

8

The arrival of the first major snowstorm of the season found Vladimir Radchenko safely ensconced inside the cozy confines of his personal railcar. Since his last visit to this same carriage, it had been moved to a sheltered siding, directly adjoining the Strategic Rocket Forces base at Art'om.

Radchenko had arrived there only that morning, after a long, tiring flight from Moscow. His Il-76 transport had landed in Vladivostok in the midst of a virtual blizzard, and he knew that he was very fortunate to have arrived in one piece.

Both Viktor Sorokin and Boris Arbatov were waiting for him at the airport. A tracked army transporter was needed to navigate the snow and convey them to Art'om. It was during the difficult drive that followed that he was able to brief his aides on the latest political intrigues taking place inside the Kremlin.

In Radchenko's opinion, their movement was extremely close to assuming total control of the government. The opposition was all but crumbling, mostly as a result of their having to lift the state of martial law because of overwhelming popular pressure. There was no doubt in Radchenko's mind that the people were ready to back their efforts, and they needed only one more element to consolidate their power. Of course, both Radchenko and his advisors were well aware of just what the missing element was, and the purpose of his current trip was to obtain it once and for all.

Only minutes earlier, Viktor Sorokin had telephoned with exciting news. Though he wouldn't reveal all of it, Radchenko could assume from the former defense minister's tone that something very exciting had just occurred. Sorokin ended their enigmatic conversation with a promise that someone would be arriving at the railcar shortly to deliver personally the information withheld.

To prepare for this visit, Radchenko stoked the glowing coals of the railcar's potbellied stove. Just in case a celebration was indeed in order, he made certain that a magnum of champagne was on ice.

A powerful gust of wind momentarily shook the carriage. There would be no innocent hikes into the surrounding woods on this frigid evening, and he felt sorry for the poor soldiers who had outdoor duty. For this was a Siberian cold that chilled one right down to the bone!

Doing his best to ignore the throbbing arthritic pains that were aggravated by the storm and made the mere act of putting on a sweater painful, he tidied up his temporary home in anticipation of his visitors. The rail carriage had originally been refurbished for tourism purposes. Rich walnut paneling graced its walls, with plush, dark red carpets and similarly colored, velveteen upholstered furniture displaying an almost Czarist opulence. A king-size Murphy bed and a small desk and chair completed the furnishings, and Radchenko made little use of the compact, well-stocked kitchen except for drinks and snacks.

A firm knock on the thick, metal door announced his company. Radchenko was surprised to find this visitor to be a single woman in a long, white sable coat and matching hat. He invited her in, ever aware of the penetrating Arctic air that also entered. Quickly sealing the door behind her, Radchenko silently appraised this newcomer. She couldn't be a day over thirty, and her face was exquisitely formed. He sensed Oriental heritage in her dark, slightly slanted eyes, and pronounced, high cheekbones. She had a delicate nose, sensual, pouting lips, and white skin, appearing as unblemished as the finest Minsk china.

"And here I was expecting that old dog Viktor Sorokin," greeted Radchenko a bit nervously. "Whom do I have the honor of addressing? May I hang up that beautiful coat of yours?"

His gorgeous visitor teasingly smiled. "If it's alright with you, Comrade Radchenko, I'll hold on to my coat for the moment. I'm Lieutenant Tanya Markova, formerly with the intelligence branch of the Strategic Rocket services."

Radchenko shook her tiny hand and found it surprisingly warm and incredibly smooth. He tried his best to be polite and not stare at her, but her innocent beauty was such that he was all but enthralled.

"Lieutenant Markova," he managed, "to what do I owe the pleasure of your presence?"

"I've come here on the express directive of comrades Sorokin and Arbatov, sir,'' she reported with strict military efficiency.

"Yes, my dear,'' anxiously replied Radchenko, his curiosity piqued.

A teasing gleam flashed in her dark eyes as she sauntered over to the potbellied stove and turned to face him once more. Only when she was certain that she had his undivided attention did she remove her hat. With carefree abandon, she tossed it onto the kitchen table, then shook loose a wild mane of long red hair. Radchenko's pulse quickened as she next began slowly unbuttoning her coat.

"You know, maybe I will let you hang up this fur after all,'' she cooed.

Before he could respond to this, she yanked open the flaps of her coat, revealing a perfectly formed, nude body. Never before had Radchenko seen such firm, pert breasts and such a tight, compact waistline. And, of course, there were those long, shapely legs, that perfectly displayed the triangular, bushy red pubic patch that hinted at great delights hidden within.

Strangely enough, she had a red silk ribbon tied around her neck, giving her the appearance of a living present. Only after she finally broke the silence did he understand that her presence was indeed a gift in many more ways than one.

"It is my proud duty to inform you, Comrade Radchenko, that as of midnight this evening, the launch codes to the Art'om strategic missile complex are ours, to do with as we please. So I certainly hope that you've got some champagne on ice, because it's time to raise our glasses in toast to the success of the greatest people's movement in the history of Mother Russia!''

It took less than twenty-four hours for ground-based U.S. intelligence assets to learn about Radchenko's compromise of the Art'om ICBM field's release codes. So important was the news that the president was awakened from a sound sleep and a crisis meeting convened in the subterranean White House situation room less than forty-five minutes later.

The meeting's consensus was to look at the release code compromise as a potential act of war. As commander-in-chief, the president personally notified the Pentagon's National Military Command Center to set a defense condition of DEFCON Three. This order was immediately instituted, and the three arms of the country's nuclear triad were alerted. The airborne assets of this triad included an aging fleet of B-52Gs and the untested B-2 Stealth bomber. America's silo-based Minuteman ICBMs were also prepared for possible launch.

The most survivable leg of the triad was unquestionably America's fleet of Ohio-class Trident submarines. Equipped with over half of the country's available nuclear warheads, the Tridents' great range, payload capability, and remarkable accuracy made them a force not to be taken lightly.

Of all the Tridents currently on patrol, it was the USS *Alabama* that was in the perfect position to hit the Art'om ICBM field. To pass on the major change in alert status to DEFCON Three, an E-6A TACAMO jet aircraft out of Barber's Point, Hawaii, was directed to overfly the *Alabama*'s patrol zone. With its name derived from the acronym for Take Charge And Move Out, the TACAMO's airframe was based on a military version of the civilian 707 airliner.

To contact the submerged submarine, a trailing wire antenna over six miles long, with a drogue parachute on its end, was deployed from a drum in the TACAMO's tail. A tight circular turn caused this antenna to dangle vertically, with a 200-kw transmitter utilized to broadcast a continuous very-low-frequency (VLF) radio transmission.

Because such a VLF signal could only penetrate the first fifty feet of water, the *Alabama* was outfitted with a 1,673-foot-long wire antenna, with a cross-looped antenna built into a specially designed buoy. At low speeds, this buoy floated upward to within the proper VLF receipt envelope.

It was during just such a routine VLF scan that Petty Officer Russell Vossler monitored the receipt of the TACAMO's broadcast. The Emergency Action Message that soon filled his monitor screen quickly gained his attention, and as he activated the printer to make a hard copy of the EAM, he immediately informed the captain.

Frank Ramsey was in the *Alabama*'s navigation station when Vossler's urgent intercom page reached him. Without a moment's hesitation, Ramsey dropped the bathymetric chart that he had been studying and took off for the nearby radio room.

It only took a cursory glance at the page-long document for Ramsey to know the utter importance of the communiqué. Before sharing its shocking contents with the rest of the crew, standard operating procedure prompted him first to show the

EAM to his XO in the radio room's OPCON. From there Hunter arranged an official crew briefing in the wardroom.

Ten minutes later, a mixed crowd of division heads, senior chiefs, and junior officers were assembled in the wardroom. Hunter began the briefing by reading the entire EAM aloud. A moment of stunned silence followed, and the XO somberly repeated the message's highlights.

"Since intel now indicates that Radchenko's forces have compromised the launch codes, we have been ordered to retarget our warheads in accordance with the National Military Command Center's decision to set an alert state of DEFCON Three."

"As many of you well know," interjected Ramsey, "only two times before have U.S. strategic forces been called to DEFCON Three, which is only a hair-trigger pull away from the actual release of nuclear weapons. The first time took place three decades ago, during the Cuban missile crisis. The last call to DEFCON Three occurred during the 1972 Arab-Israeli Yom Kippur War."

Making it a point to halt and scan the stunned faces of his audience, Ramsey added, "Gentlemen, this is what we have trained for. It's why this ship was built, and the reason we carry along those twenty-four Trident missiles.

"The NCA has determined that should our satellites detect that rebel missiles are being fueled, which means that they can be launched in just over one hour, we will be compelled to act. So it's clear that our friends in the Pentagon are setting us up for a potential preemptive strike."

In response to his last revelation, a wave of concerned chatter escaped the lips of those present. Ramsey briefly met his XO's glance, then raised his arms overhead to silence his audience.

"I'll be personally addressing the crew over the 1MC to share our new mission. I'm certain that their response will be much like your own, and I'm counting on all of you to answer their questions and ease any anxieties that they might have. Of course, both the XO and I are always available should you have any questions yourselves. Please don't hesitate to approach either one of us. That is all, men. Dismissed."

As anticipated, the general announcement of the *Alabama*'s new alert status was received with great unease. This was particularly the case with the junior-most enlisted men, whose experiences on stategic missile deterrent patrols were limited.

For the first couple of days after the announcement was made, the boat's chiefs and officers were busy counseling those sailors who had trouble accepting the reality of their current situation. Their apprehensions surfaced in nightmares and bouts of insomnia. Spirited discussions raged throughout the ship, covering the horrors of a global nuclear war and just what the results would be for their loved ones back home. For men who had been raised in a post–Cold War climate, nuclear conflict had been something that they merely trained for. Yet the reality that their training might very well be called upon to initiate the unthinkable dawned in their minds the moment the *Alabama*'s captain informed them of their latest alert status.

Further aggravating the crew's sense of unease was the fact that they were some three weeks into their patrol. In normal circumstances that would be approaching a patrol's halfway point. That was usually when morale was at its lowest, and nerves the most strained. The lack of privacy and close living quarters were particularly hard to cope with, as was demonstrated by a minor incident that took place in the crew's berthing space number twelve.

Set on the port side of the third level missile compartment, berthing space twelve was located directly opposite the crew's study. It was home to nine enlisted men, one of whom was chief sonarman Danny Rivetti.

Rivetti was off duty and wasn't due back in the sonar room for another two hours. He had just awoken from a sound slumber and planned to remain in his rack and read until mid-rats were served in thirty minutes.

As he flicked on the overhead fluorescent light, he surveyed his private domain. His bunk was just long enough to hold his five-foot, ten-inch frame, and turning over always proved a challenge. But at the very least this cramped space was his to do with as he wished, and now that he had his curtains pulled shut, his privacy could be assured.

Most of his clothing was stored in a narrow locker directly beneath his mattress. A small metal box at the foot of his bunk and several cloth pockets for items such as his slippers, watch, flashlight, and snacks held the rest of his personal belongings. Though it wasn't much to brag about, it was all his, and he had even managed to add some atmosphere to these cramped confines.

Lining the walls on three sides of his bunk, was a 360-degree, panoramic view of the downtown Manhattan skyline. The original photograph had been taken from the top deck of the Staten Island ferry, and Danny had found it in a Bronx poster shop.

Until his enlistment in the navy three years ago, New York City had been the exclusive extent of his world. He was born and raised in the Williamsburg section of Brooklyn, right down the street from the old Brooklyn Navy Yard.

In such an environment he grew up tough, wise in the ways of the street and its people. His close family helped keep him out of serious trouble, and he even managed to complete high school, with his dream to one day become a professional musician.

Even though he never became proficient on an instrument, his love of music got him a job at a basement recording studio on Division Avenue. It was there he learned the business of music and decided that his best chance at making a living in the music field was to become a recording engineer.

To get such a position, college was a must. With seven mouths to feed at home, his father suggested that Danny should think about enlisting in the armed forces and take advantage of the GI Bill to earn his tuition. It was something that he had never considered before, and since his father was a veteran of the navy, he decided to give the same service a try.

The local recruiter had only just arrived in the area after a six-year-long stint as a master chief aboard a nuclear attack sub. He was extremely personable, and it was during the interview that followed that Danny first learned about the vital importance of sound to a submariner. A month later he was on his way to basic training in San Diego, where he planned to become a sonar specialist on a nuclear submarine.

He attained his goal and much more. Danny became a man of the world. Since graduating sub school he had traveled to many an exotic port and couldn't begin to count the many new friends from all over the country with whom he had sailed.

If all went as planned, he would leave the navy in three more years. Taking along the skills he had learned as a sonar operator, he'd attend college at night, all the while searching for full-time employment in a recording studio. If the world didn't self-destruct in the meantime, he was more confident than ever of attaining his goal.

Wishing that he could get on a telephone and let his pop know how well he was doing, Danny pulled a well-worn paperback out of his rack's storage pocket. He decided to also extract his portable Discman. It was loaded with a CD entitled "Songs of the Humpback Whale." Certainly no stranger to the melodious, bewitching natural sound track that was soon filling his ears, he immersed himself in the story that he was more than half finished with.

It had been a shipmate who originally lent him the novel. It was proving to be a well-written, fast-moving techno-thriller. The strange plot concerned a group of modern-day Neo-Nazis who were using a World War II–era Type XXI U-boat to travel to Antarctica and retrieve a legendary treasure containing the occult secrets of the Third Reich. The plot was really getting interesting now that the crew of an American 688I attack sub was getting involved in the action.

He read for well over an hour, only stopping

when the CD finally ended. As he slipped off the headphones, his sensitive ears picked up the distinctive, thumping sound of a powerful bass beat nearby. He knew in an instant precisely where the nerve-racking background noise was coming from, for he had heard such a racket on many previous occasions.

Danny put down his book, turned on his side, and ripped open his curtains. It only took a quick peek at the occupied rack set immediately beneath his to know that Seaman Bennefield had most likely fallen asleep with his Walkman blaring away at full volume again. He confirmed this fact by parting the curtains and looking inside. As expected, Bennefield was sprawled out on his back cutting Zs. The crew-cut, blond-haired Californian was a self-avowed surfer boy, and his tall, muscular body seemed to fill up the entire bunk. Even though his Walkman's headphones were tightly clamped over his ears, there could be no missing the racket that still managed to leak out.

Unable to summon the patience just to return to his rack and try to ignore the pounding rock bass line, Danny decided on a direct frontal assault. To rid himself of the aggravation, he reached down and boldly switched off the Walkman's power.

No sooner did he hit the off button than Bennefield's eyes snapped open. A confused look filled the young Californian's blue eyes. Yet this look quickly turned to disbelief, and finally to pure anger, as he realized the exact nature of his bunkmate's indiscretion.

''Damn it, Rivetti! Just what in the hell do you think you're doing?''

Danny was well prepared for just such a reaction on Bennefield's part, and he came back just as hard. "For God's sake, Bennefield! I could hear that poor excuse for music that you were feeding into your brain all the way up in my rack. Have a little courtesy, man!"

"Courtesy?" shot back Bennefield. "Who the hell was it that had the balls to reach in here and fool with my private belongings? You damn pushy New Yorkers are all alike!"

With this, he defiantly switched his Walkman back on. Danny lost it at that point and, seething with rage, jumped out of his rack and yanked the headphones right out of Bennefield's ears.

It had been a missing missile drill report that had initially sent Hunter down to the COB's office. Ever thankful to get a chance to stretch his legs after a paperwork marathon had kept him bolted to his desk, Hunter climbed down to the third level and headed aft, through the missile compartment.

The hour was late, and there was a noticeable lack of personnel present as he approached the crew's study. The COB's office directly adjoined this room, and it was as Hunter prepared to enter the study that the sound of a scuffle drew him through the drawn curtains of berthing space number twelve.

Hunter wasn't prepared for that which he found taking place there. Dressed solely in his skivvies, Chief Sonarman Danny Rivetti was in the process of duking it out with a tall, muscular sailor that Hunter knew only as Bennefield. Hunter could see that they weren't just horsing around and he quickly interceded.

"Gentlemen, stop this nonsense now!" he shouted.

Thankfully, they listened to him. And as both combatants lowered their fists, Hunter added.

"What in the hell is all this about?"

Danny Rivetti answered apologetically. "I'm sorry, sir. It was just a little music disagreement that got out of hand."

Hunter suspected that there was much more to the story than this. Yet both combatants appeared to be appeased. And since no punches had actually been landed, Hunter summarily dismissed them with a strict warning and an invitation for Rivetti to join him in the crew's study.

The dozen-or-so individual cubicles that made up the study were mercifully vacant as Hunter entered. Rivetti followed seconds later, now dressed in his poopy suit and looking every bit like a guilty puppy.

"Now what the hell was all that about, Rivetti?"

Danny looked embarrassed as he searched for the words to express himself. "I'm really sorry, sir. It's just that Bennefield was playing his Walkman at full volume, and that bass line was driving me crazy!"

"But is that any reason to start a fight with one of your shipmates?" Hunter argued. "You're a goddamn supervisor, son. From what I've already seen of your work, you're the best sonarman we've got, and I wouldn't even rule out a commission in your future. But to throw all of that away because you don't like the volume of a guy's music just doesn't make sense."

Rivetti sheepishly replied. "I hear you loud and

clear, sir. I lost it, pure and simple. If you've got to write this up, I take full responsibility.''

Hunter sensed the intelligent youngster's shame, and he instinctively softened his tone. ''No, son, I'm not gonna write you up this time. But if I ever see this bullshit come down again, your ass is mine!''

Certain that he had gotten his point across, Hunter turned his back on Rivetti, and continued on to the COB's nearby office. After a knock on the closed door failed to generate a response, he discreetly turned the knob and entered the vacant office that was little more than a cluttered cubicle. He found the report that he was looking for sitting in the COB's ''out'' basket. Beside this basket was the partially completed wooden model of a sailboat. It was superbly crafted, and it was most apparent that quite a lot of time and effort had gone into its construction. Totally unaware that the COB had such a hobby, Hunter left the office to return to his stateroom.

This time he climbed up to the deck above by way of the aft accessway. This put him in the after end of the mid-level missile compartment where he ran. Already looking forward to the next day's jog, he was caught by surprise when the *Alabama*'s captain suddenly emerged from the tubes set immediately in front of him. Ramsey held Bear by his leash and had a well-chewed-on rubber ball in the palm of his other hand.

''Good evening, Mr. Hunter,'' greeted Ramsey nonchalantly.

Momentarily caught off guard by this unexpected meeting, Hunter quickly recovered. ''Good evening, sir. I have those missile drill results that you asked for earlier.''

Ramsey casually traded Bear's leash for the report that Hunter had just pulled from the COB's office. Hunter briefly traded glances with Bear. They'd finally accepted each other as shipmates.

"Is this the best they can do?" Ramsey asked, after reading the drill results.

"No, sir. But that's what they did."

"I want that retargeting sequence down to five minutes," demanded Ramsey as he disgustedly handed the report back to Hunter and took back Bear's leash. "Train on it. And tell your buddy Weps that we're gonna do it again, and keep on doing it, until he gets it right. Damn, right now it feels like the whole crew needs a good kick in the ass.''

"Or a pat on the head, sir," Hunter countered.

His remark got Ramsey's full attention, and his XO defiantly added, "I just had to break up a little fight down in crew berthing. Two good men were fighting over pure bullshit. It's only too obvious that the crew's a bit on edge from what we're going through right now, and, as a result, morale's suffering."

"You don't say," quipped Ramsey, his sarcasm obvious. "Well, Mr. Hunter, since you obviously have the pulse of the men, I'd better have a word with them."

Hunter could hardly believe it as Ramsey went over to the nearest intercom handset and addressed the entire crew over the 1MC.

"May I have your attention, please? This is your captain. Mr. Hunter has just brought it to my attention that morale may be a bit low. He feels that you may be a bit on edge. So what I suggest is this. Any crew member who feels that he can't handle this situation can leave the ship right now! Gentlemen, I hope that I still don't have to remind you, but we are at DEFCON Three. That is all.''

With a self-satisfied smirk, Ramsey clicked off the 1MC and turned to face his XO. A moment of chilling silence followed, and it was Hunter who finally broke it.

''Very inspiring, Captain. Yet may I ask what ever happened to airing all differences of opinion in private?''

With that said, Hunter stormed off to his stateroom, his pulse racing and stomach tight. By the time he finally reached his quarters, he was feeling emotionally and physically drained. Unable to focus his scrambled thoughts, he lay down on his cot and surrendered to an almost instant slumber.

He awoke four and a half hours later, feeling unusually rested and fresh. As he showered and shaved, he recreated each moment of his latest confrontation with Frank Ramsey. They seemed to be drifting farther apart with each passing day, and Hunter could only wonder how long it would be until their stormy relationship finally reached its breaking point.

After checking his calendar, he found that he had just enough time to grab a cup of coffee and a doughnut before his first scheduled appointment of the day was due to arrive. This long-delayed meeting promised to be a somewhat awkward one, and Hunter would be more than happy when it was finally over.

He returned to his stateroom with coffee cup in hand just as the COB was emerging from the second level's aft port passageway. Hunter spotted the portly, crew-cut chief of the boat as he rounded the doorway leading to the ship's office, and he warmly raised his voice in greeting.

"You're right on time, COB. Would you like to grab some coffee before we begin?"

"That's quite all right, sir. I've already had my morning caffeine fix."

Hunter escorted his guest into his quarters and shut the door behind them. He beckoned the COB to grab one of the room's two chairs, and Hunter sat down beside him.

"First off, COB, I've got to 'fess up to a minor charge of breaking and entering. During last night's mid-watch I had to raid your office to get a copy of that latest missile drill report."

"Any apology on your part isn't necessary, sir. In fact, I'm the one who should be asking for forgiveness. That report should have been on your desk a good two hours earlier."

"You know, I couldn't help but notice that model sailboat on your desk. Is that your work, Chief?"

The COB proudly nodded. "That it is, sir. She's a Falmouth Cutter, and a sweeter surface boat there's not on all the seven seas."

"Is model building something that you always do while on patrol?" asked Hunter, satisfied to have successfully broken the ice.

"Aye, sir. When I do manage to wrangle some free time, there's nothin' like a hobby to keep you out of trouble."

Knowing full well what this trouble was in the COB's instance, Hunter did his diplomatic best to change the tack of their discussion and focus in on the delicate subject that determined the meeting's primary agenda. "COB, I know this is difficult, but while reading your fitness report . . ."

The COB saved Hunter any further embarrassment by quickly chiming in. "Maybe I can help, sir. I know I'm overweight, and that I've had two official cautionary notes. This gut's part thyroid, and a good part indulgence. But this is my last tour. I plan to retire shortly and sail off in the twenty-foot sloop that model's based upon."

Hunter suddenly realized that it really wasn't the COB's weight problem that he wanted to talk about and he drastically changed course again. "I'm certain that you heard the captain's little impromptu speech to the crew earlier."

"Yes, I did, sir."

"Well, Chief, what did you think of it?"

The COB didn't hesitate. "I think the captain just seems to know what his men really need."

"Yeah, a pat on the head or a kick in the ass," interjected Hunter.

"Sir, with all due respect, his speech sure made good sense to me."

Hunter tried his best to keep his mind open as the *Alabama*'s senior-most enlisted man continued.

"This thing between you and the captain is no good for morale. Somebody's gotta bend, sir, and he's the skipper."

"I believe I'm aware of that fact," snapped Hunter, who knew it was time to clear the air.

"Okay, go ahead, COB. You've got the floor. No rank and no punches pulled."

The chief anxiously sat forward and got down to business. "I think what we have here is a difference in management styles. As unpredictable as he might be, there's a certain logic to it. The skipper navigates by his own star. Not many people can do that."

Halting briefly to let this observation sink in, he added, "COB's rules of navy leadership—One: you gotta look like you know what you're doing. Two: your men have gotta believe you know what you're doing. And third, and most important of all: everybody else gets to have an opinion. But it's the captain that has to make a choice. You live and die with that. That's where the skipper's earned his stripes. I've seen it time and time again."

Hunter interrupted. "So, when you're right, you're right, huh?"

"That's what my daddy used to say," reflected the COB with a fond grin. "Right's right, and wrong's for nobody."

Vladimir Radchenko was awakened by the distant crackle of gunfire. The distinctive reports seemed to intensify as he sat up stiffly and wiped the sleep from his eyes. Beside him on the king-size bed, beneath the thick, goose-down comforter, Tanya Markova slept soundly, oblivious to the muted, worrisome racket coming from outside.

She appeared so very innocent in her slumber, her luscious lips barely parted and invitingly beckoning. But Radchenko knew that beneath her angelic veneer was the spirit of a lust-filled demon. Just looking at her sleeping caused his shrunken member to stiffen. She had shared his bed each and every night since that fated first evening when they met. And what a wonderful lover she proved to be—soft, responsive, and not too demanding.

How very unlike she was to his Anna. His wife of thirty years waited for him back in Tiskovo. Though Anna was a splendid cook and a spotless housekeeper, the sexual spark of their love life had long since been extinguished. For the first time in years, the primal urge of sexual longing filled his loins, and it was almost like getting a chance to relive his youth once more. Ever thankful for Tanya's presence, he rose from the bed to see what the persistent gunfire was all about.

The interior of the railcar was chilly, and after wrapping himself in a terry cloth robe and burying his feet in woolen slippers, he stoked the coals in the potbellied stove. As he headed into the small kitchen, he passed the empty vodka bottles and partially filled appetizer trays from the previous night's party. A butt-filled ashtray lay on the counter, and he guiltily reached for a nearby pack of Dunhill cigarettes. Two nights ago he had finally broken down and begun smoking once more. Promising himself that he'd limit his consumption to a pack a day and then quit once this nerve-racking crisis was over, he lit up one of the English cigarettes.

It was as he inhaled his first lungful of the strong, fragrant tobacco, that a muffled explosion outside rattled the interior of the train carriage. Radchenko worriedly headed for his paper-cluttered desk, where a field telephone was set up.

His call found Viktor Sorokin inside the missile base's subterranean control room. Radchenko merely had to hear the breathless, apprehensive manner in which his aide addressed him to know that something bad was occurring.

"Ah, Vladimir Ilyich, I was just about to call you myself," revealed the former defense minister.

"What the hell is all that gunfire about, Viktor? It sounds like there's a full-scale war going on out there."

"Believe me, Comrade. It's really nothing we can't handle. It appears that we caught a group of loyalist Spetsnaz sappers trying to burrow beneath the south gate. I've ordered the security response squad in to block their efforts, and that racket you're hearing is only the sound of our cleanup operation.''

Radchenko grunted skeptically. ''I certainly hope that's the extent of it, Viktor. My greatest fear remains the consolidation of our opponents' forces, and we must be absolutely positive that the presence of those sappers isn't the start of a major offensive to retake the base.''

''You know my feeling on that matter, Comrade,'' replied Sorokin firmly. ''The loyalist forces are in total disarray and couldn't mount an attack even if they wanted. No, I believe that the sappers are only probing our defenses and that their presence only shows how weak and desperate our opponents really are.''

After a brief pause, Sorokin added, ''More significant than this isolated firefight are the potential implications of a recent flight through our airspace, Vladimir Ilyich. The incident took place less than an hour ago, when our radar screens picked up a single, unidentified, high-altitude aircraft approaching Art'om from the northeast. I immediately ordered a pair of MiG-25s to intercept this bogey, but unfortunately it managed to evade our fighters and escape.''

''How very interesting,'' Radchenko reflected. ''And the identity of this intruder, Viktor?''

''From the preliminary description of our lead MiG pilot, I'm almost positive that it was an American SR-71 spy plane.''

This news enraged Radchenko, and he spit

smoke from the clenched Dunhill as he shouted his response. "So now even the Americans want to get involved in our affairs! We should have expected such an aggressive move on their part, and now it's time to show them that we mean business. Notify the Akulas that they're free to engage any enemy submarines that dare approach our shores and instruct the technicians to begin fueling the missiles. The time has arrived for Russia to stand tall and be a great power once again!"

Approximately two thousand miles due east of the strategic missile base at Art'om, the USS *Alabama* cut silently through the deep waters surrounding the Emperor Seamount chain. Inside the sub's 560-foot-long hull, the crew went about their duties totally unaware of the political intrigues that were about to change their destinies.

It was business as usual as Senior Sonar Supervisor Danny Rivetti settled in for a six-hour watch. The team that his had just relieved reported the presence of whales in the vicinity, and Rivetti hoped that these boisterous mammals of the deep would also pay his watch a visit.

With his altercation with Seaman Bennefield still bothering him, Rivetti promised himself that he'd never again lose his temper over such a minor, trivial matter. Still not certain what had possessed him to act so aggressively, he knew that he was very fortunate to be serving under such an understanding XO as Lieutenant Commander Hunter. The XO could have easily written him up for his outburst, and years of dedicated hard work could have gone down the drain as a result.

Hunter's mention that he thought Danny had the right stuff to be an officer was particularly flattering. Though gaining such a commission wasn't his original goal when he enlisted, it was something he decided to consider seriously now that the XO had mentioned his potential.

Danny Rivetti—an officer and a gentleman! Why he could just see the faces of his family and friends back in Brooklyn when he strolled up to their brownstone in officer's blues. How very proud they'd be!

Laughing to himself at the foolishness of this lofty thought, Danny reached up into the overhead vent to prepare the day's treats. If his boys behaved themselves, he'd be distributing individually wrapped, bite-sized Snickers bars. Of course, Snickers was also his favorite candy, and he wondered what he'd have to do to be worthy of sharing one of these treats himself.

"Sup," said the sailor responsible for monitoring their towed array, "I think you'd better take a look at this."

Rivetti set his practiced gaze on the sailor's CRT screen. He immediately spotted a small flutter in the monitor's waterfall display. And just as he was wondering whether or not the irregularity could be an anomaly, the sonarman seated at the far right console barked out, "I have a broadband contact bearing zero-four-seven, tracking A-one-nine-eight hertz. Assigning tracker Sierra in ATF and AFT."

Rivetti's hand shot out for his headphones. He securely placed them over his ears and hurriedly addressed the keyboard belonging to the broadband processor. Seconds later, a wave of static-filled noise filled his headphones. He readdressed the keyboard to engage the graphic equalizer and the static faded, to be replaced with a barely audible, pulsating, throbbing sound, that caused him to gasp in instant recognition.

"Conn, sonar!" he yelled into the intercom. "We have a submerged contact, bearing zero-four-seven. Designate Sierra two-eight, possible hostile submarine!"

Hunter was in the missile control center with Weps, discussing the manner in which they could shave some time off the next missile drill, when the dreaded announcement arrived over the 1MC.

"Man battle stations torpedo! Rig for ultra quiet!"

Well aware that they had no such drill on the schedule, he left Weps with a concerned glance and took off at once for the control room. It was at the forward stairway that he encounted the captain. Ramsey was in the process of exiting his stateroom and appeared to have just awoken from a deep sleep. This almost assured that this alert was in fact not a drill, and Hunter allowed his CO to lead the way up to the control room on the deck above.

Arriving in the conn, they found Lieutenant Linkletter to be the current officer of the deck. The *Alabama*'s tactical systems operator was certainly in his element as he organized the fire control tracking party and readied the boat's response to any possible threat that awaited them in the seas beyond.

"Make tubes one and four fully ready," Linkletter ordered.

"What have you got, Mr. Linkletter?" asked

Ramsey as he joined the OOD on the periscope pedestal.

"Sir, sonar reports a possible submerged submarine. Bearing zero-four-seven. Designate Sierra two-eight at outer envelope of range perimeter."

Hunter arrived on the slightly raised platform in time to hear Ramsey's next question.

"What's the best depth for evasion?"

"The latest bathymetric probe indicated a pronounced thermal layer at 830 feet, sir."

Ramsey displayed a remarkable degree of composure as he turned and calmly addressed Chief Hunsicker, the ship's current diving officer.

"Chief Hunsicker, increase speed to standard. Come left to course two-seven-zero. Make your depth eight-three-zero feet."

As the diving officer repeated the captain's instructions and began implementing them, Ramsey turned his attention to his XO.

"Mr. Hunter, I want you in sonar to find out who the hell's out there!"

"Aye, sir."

Hunter smartly began his way forward. He passed by the helmsmen as they were in the process of pushing down hard on their yokes. By the time he reached the nearby sonar room, the deck was already angling down by the bow, and he had to compensate carefully to keep from being pitched headfirst into the forward bulkhead.

Once inside the dimly lit, hushed confines of sonar, Hunter was able to stabilize himself by grabbing onto an overhead, steel-looped handhold. He couldn't have been happier to find Danny Rivetti on duty as the current sonar supervisor. Rivetti was huddled over the narrowband processor, deftly addressing its keyboard.

"Can you identify Sierra two-eight, Sup?" Hunter hopefully asked.

Rivetti answered without taking his eyes off the waterfall display. "I'm tryin' my best, sir. I'm tryin' my best."

Directly across the passageway from sonar was the *Alabama*'s radio room. Caught off guard by the sub's sudden, deeply angled descent, Roy Zimmer found himself on his hands and knees trying to retrieve a fallen code book. Somehow the thin volume had managed to slide beneath the bottom portion of the printer, forcing him to grope for it blindly. Several frustrating attempts finally paid off, and just as he gripped the notebook and pulled it out, his assistant's voice rang out from the main console.

"Hot damn, Lieutenant!" exclaimed Russell Vossler. "We've got us an EAM!"

Zimmer struggled to his feet and fought off the steep angle of the deck to make his way over to the console. What he saw on the monitor screen caused his eyes to open wide, and he wasted no time notifying the control room via the intercom.

"Conn, radio. We are receiving an Emergency Action Message. Recommend alert one!"

Momentarily putting aside the intercom handset, Zimmer spoke to his assistant. "Run the rest of that message through the decrypting device."

Vossler did as ordered. Slowly the monitor screen began filling with the decoded transmission, and as Vossler read it, his faced turned pale.

"Oh, fuck!" he cursed, his tone heavy with fear.

"Keep it cool, son," Zimmer advised, while reaching out to activate the printer.

With a hard copy version of the message in his trembling hands, Zimmer turned for the adjoining OPCON. Ramsey, Hunter, and Darik Westerguard met him there.

"Captain," said Zimmer as he showed the dispatch to Westerguard, "it appears that we've just received a properly formatted Emergency Action Message from the National Command Authority."

Pausing to catch his breath, he added incredulously, "For strategic missile launch!"

"I concur, sir," managed Westerguard, his voice warbling, his face ashen.

Ramsey grabbed the message. As he read it, Hunter found himself watching for any signs in the captain's expression that might hint that this whole thing was nothing but a drill, and that the two junior officers had somehow misinterpreted the EAM.

"Captain, request permission to authenticate," Zimmer asked.

"Permission granted," returned Ramsey. "Get the authenticator."

Hunter noted how Zimmer's hands were shaking as he went to the OPCON's main safe and began turning its dial. It took him two attempts to finally open it. Westerguard was able to access the inner safe with a single attempt, and he quickly removed the sealed packet holding the authenticator card. With his hands still shaking, Zimmer tore open the packet, removed the card, and held it up against the EAM.

"Bravo, Echo, Echo, Charlie, Alpha, Tango, Alpha," revealed Zimmer.

"Bravo, Echo, Echo, Charlie, Alpha, Tango, Alpha," Westerguard repeated as he checked the authenticator himself.

Zimmer looked up, a stunned expression on his face. "The message is authentic, sir."

"I agree, Captain," said Westerguard.

At that point Hunter grabbed the authenticator to double-check their work. Much to his utter amazement, the codes matched. "Sir, I also concur," he concluded somberly.

Only after checking the authenticator himself, did Ramsey coolly speak. "Gentlemen, this message is authentic. Mr. Hunter, Mr. Westerguard, if you'll please join me in control, we'll get on with implementing it."

Hunter followed Ramsey back into the control room. If a space that cramped could somehow feel smaller to Hunter, it did then. There was almost a nightmarish quality to the sequence of events that followed as he watched Ramsey notify the crew.

"Chief of the Watch, secure from battle stations torpedo. Man battle stations missiles for strategic launch. Spin up all missiles!"

Chief Hunsicker was forced to do a double take upon hearing this unexpected command. Ramsey appeared to be waiting for just such a reaction from the grizzled veteran, and he calmly repeated the order. Hunsicker had to hear no more to address the crew over the 1MC.

"Secure from battle stations torpedo. Man battle stations missile for strategic launch. Spin up all missiles!"

The general alarm began bonging away in the background. It sounded throughout the ship for nineteen eerie seconds, announcing the arrival of Armageddon to the crew of the USS *Alabama*.

With the boat still in the midst of its descent beneath the thermocline, Hunter joined Ramsey behind the captain's missile indicator panel. From this central position they had a clear view of the rapidly falling numbers of the helm's digital depth gauge. Along with the authenticator card, Lieutenant Zimmer had removed a single key from the sealed packet. This key was now secured to the leather lanyard that hung around Ramsey's neck and was the only way to unlock the indicator panel and initiate the launch sequence from this vantage point.

No sooner did the general alarm stop bonging than Ramsey pulled out his stopwatch and reached up for the overhead PA microphone. "Weapons, conn. Set condition 1SQ for strategic missile launch. Spin up missiles one through five and twenty through twenty-four. The release of nuclear weapons has been authorized. Gentlemen, this is not a drill. This is the captain."

Hunter alertly grabbed the microphone to repeat this order. "Weapons, conn. Set condition 1SQ for strategic missile launch. Spin up missiles one through five and twenty through twenty-four. The release of nuclear weapons has been authorized. This is the XO."

Hunter's throat was unnaturally dry as he hung up the microphone. Beside him, Ramsey didn't look the least bit affected as he casually handed Hunter the EAM.

"Mr. Hunter, please take the conn in my absence. I'm going to my stateroom to remove the ten firing unit keys from my safe."

Hunter acknowledged his request with the barest of nods. He watched vacantly as Ramsey left the control room, then reread the EAM.

XREEBABA . . . . . . EMERGENCY ACTION MESSAGE (300)

FROM: NATIONAL MILITARY COMMAND CENTER
TO: USS ALABAMA (SSBN 731)
SUBJECT: NUCLEAR MISSILE LAUNCH—SINGLE
INTEGRATED OPERATIONAL PLAN (SIOP)
EXECUTION.
REMARKS: REBEL-CONTROLLED MISSILES BEING
FUELED. LAUNCH CODES
COMPROMISED. DISSIDENTS THREATEN
LAUNCH AT CONTINENTAL UNITED
STATES.

1. SET DEFCON TWO.
2. RETARGET AND STRIKE.
3. IMMEDIATE LAUNCH TEN (10) TRIDENT MISSILE
SORTIES.
4. TARGET PACKAGE SLBM 64741/2.
5. AUTHENTICATION: BRAVO ECHO ECHO
CHARLIE ALPHA TANGO ALPHA.

"Conn, weapons," broke the voice of Peter Ince over the control room's intercom. "Estimated time to 1SQ for strategic missile launch is fourteen minutes."

Thus jarred back to the present moment, Hunter put down the EAM and picked up the overhead microphone. "Weapons, conn. Aye, Mr. Ince."

"Sir, we're passing five-five-zero feet," the

COB observed from his seated position between the two helmsmen.

"Conn, radio," broke Zimmer's voice over the intercom. "We're out of VLF radio range, sir. Full message receipt capability has been cut off."

Hunter allowed his extensive training to carry him as he readdressed the microphone. "Radio, conn. Extend the Extremely Low Frequency antenna."

"Conn, radio. Extend the ELF antenna, aye, conn."

"Passing six hundred feet," informed the COB by rote. "Continuing to eight-three-zero feet, sir."

All of those assembled inside the control room got a sobering reminder about the reason for such an extreme depth change when Danny Rivetti's excited voice sounded over the intercom.

"Conn, sonar. Sierra two-eight appears to be coming down with us, bearing one-nine-six."

"Sonar, conn," spoke Hunter into the microphone. "Any hint as to the identity of Sierra two-eight, Mr. Rivetti?"

Rivetti's voice could be heard quivering as he responded to this query. "Conn, sonar. Sierra two-eight appears to correspond to the signature of a Russian Akula-class hunter-killer, sir."

This dismal piece of news arrived in the control room along with a reinvigorated Frank Ramsey.

"I should have guessed as much," spit Ramsey as he joined Hunter behind the missile indicator panel. "I still don't know how in the hell they ever tagged us, but right now, that's irrelevant."

"Approaching eight hundred feet, Captain," informed the COB.

"COB, I want you to continue our dive until I tell you otherwise," Ramsey directed.

With a look of grim determination painted on his face, Ramsey briefly glanced at Hunter before addressing the entire crew over the 1MC. "Gentlemen, this is your captain. I have just learned that we have a Russian Akula-class attack sub on our tail. We know for a fact that Vladimir Radchenko controls at least four of these submarines, and this could be one of them. These same Russian rebels have threatened to launch nuclear-tipped missiles at our country, and these missiles are fueling up right now. In response to this, we have orders to launch our Tridents, which is what we are going to do."

Pausing a moment, he added, "This is as real as it gets, gentlemen. We will presume nothing and defend ourselves at all costs. And if that Akula so much as comes around or opens a tube door, we'll take her out. That is all. Carry on."

"Passing target depth of 830 feet, Captain," interjected the COB, a hint of concern in his voice. "Shall I continue the dive, sir?"

"God damn it, COB!" cursed Ramsey. "I told you to continue this damn dive until I tell you otherwise!"

Not accustomed to being castigated in such a rude manner, the COB merely shrugged his beefy shoulders and obediently replied. "Very well, sir. Approaching 860 feet . . . 865 . . . 870 . . ."

Hunter listened to the COB's rote depth reports and all the while tried hard to understand the captain's current strategy. They were well beneath the deepest thermal layer now, and Hunter could only guess that Ramsey intended to lose the Akula in a part of the ocean's depths that it wasn't designed to operate in.

"Approaching one thousand feet," revealed the COB, who flinched as the *Alabama*'s hull plates began to creak and groan ominously.

Trying their best to ignore the sounds, the occupants of the radio room were once more called to their consoles by the beep that signaled the arrival of yet another message. The communiqué was conveyed via the vessel's Extremely Low Frequency antenna. Designed to allow the receipt of radio messages at great depths, the ELF system, though remarkably effective, was extremely slow. Because of this slow delivery rate, a three-letter code had been instituted. Some 17,500 different messages could be sent using this highly compressed code, which was called a trigraph and could take up to fifteen minutes to be delivered.

Both Roy Zimmer and Russell Vossler had their eyes glued to the ELF console screen, as the first letter began slowly materializing on the monitor. Both of them were fully aware that this broadcast originated in the far-off wilds of Michigan's upper peninsula, at K.I. Sawyer Air Force Base. Here fifty-eight miles of antennae were strung out on poles, much like telephone wires. Amazingly, this transmission site's signals could reach under the ice pack as well as such distant depths of the Pacific as the Emperor Seamount region.

With agonizing slowness, the letter Z finally formed itself on the screen, and Zimmer reached for the nearest intercom handset. "Conn, radio," he reported. "We're receiving a transmission on the Extremely Low Frequency band."

This generated an almost instantaneous response from the captain over the PA. "Radio, conn. Very well. The XO is on his way."

With the *Alabama* still in the midst of its steep descent, Hunter arrived in the radio room, his body pulled unnaturally forward, like a ski jumper at lift-off. He balanced himself using the compartment's overhead handholds and reached the ELF console just as the letter *X* appeared beside the *Z*.

"This is one hell of a time for an ELF page," observed Hunter, the hull continuing to forebodingly creak in the background.

"How much deeper are we gonna go?" Zimmer worriedly asked. "We're way beyond the normal reach of the ELF system as it is."

"Right now that decision is firmly in the hands of the captain," said Hunter.

All eyes remained locked on the flickering CRT screen. Hunter found himself silently imploring the arrival of the final letter of the trigraph. And after the longest couple of minutes of his life, a *D* finally formed itself on the monitor.

Zimmer's hands flew over the keyboard as he queried the computer to pull up the meaning of the trigraph *ZXD*. The computer processed this request, and the screen flickered alive with the answer.

EXTREMELY LOW FREQUENCY—MESSAGE CODE
ZXD: COME TO COMMUNICATIONS DEPTH TO
RECEIVE EMERGENCY ACTION MESSAGE.

Hunter's hand shot out for the intercom. "Conn, radio. We have been ordered via ELF page to come to communications depth to receive an Emergency Action Message!"

Ramsey's voice replied over the PA. "Mr. Hunter, must I remind you that we still have a suspected hostile submarine up there."

"Approaching twelve hundred feet," reported the COB's voice in the background.

His voice still amplified over the open PA channel, Ramsey replied, "COB, level us out, zero bubble."

At a depth of 1,050 feet the *Alabama* pulled out of its descent. It took another 225 feet for the helmsmen to stabilize the boat, and it was at a final depth of 1,275 feet that the deck finally leveled out.

At long last, Hunter was able to let go of the overhead handhold. Barely aware of a stinging sensation in his right palm, he listened as Ramsey's voice announced his intentions.

"When our missile system is ready, we will ascend to launch depth, release our birds, and then get the hell out. But I'm not going up until then. No way am I going to jeopardize this ship's safety."

"We could float the buoy up to comm depth from here," suggested Zimmer to the XO. "We should have just enough cable."

Hunter passed on this idea to the captain, and Ramsey immediately agreed to attempt it.

"Very well," said Ramsey over the PA. "Chief of the Watch, prepare to float the VLF buoy."

From the diving control station Chief Hunsicker activated the towed buoy antenna array. As its steel cable tether was released, the buoy inflated, causing it to shoot up toward the surface.

"Buoy deploying," informed the chief of the watch. "Tension two thousand pounds."

From his perch in the radio room, Hunter visualized the buoy's pigtail extension as it steadily bobbed upward. If all went as planned, the array would stabilize just below the sea's surface, allowing them clear access to the EAM awaiting them over the VLF frequency.

Inside the sonar compartment, Danny Rivetti also was in the process of visualizing the buoy's deployment. With his watch team focused on any signs of the Akula, Rivetti fully appreciated the precariousness of their current position. At that moment, producing any unwanted noise on the *Alabama*'s part was his greatest worry. And that very fear was realized when a deafening, metallic creak sounded outside with such volume that it could be heard without the benefit of headphones.

"Sweet Mother Mary!" Rivetti exclaimed. "Roth, pull up the internal sound compromise schematic!"

A cutaway view of the *Alabama*'s hull popped up on the monitor screen. A blinking red cursor was visible just aft of the missile magazine, and Rivetti alertly reported his findings to the control room.

"Conn, sonar. We have a sound compromise at the towed buoy antenna winch!"

Rivetti listened as the PA filled with the furious voice of the captain. "Stop the goddamn winch!"

"Winch is stopped, sir," informed the chief of the watch.

This fact was confirmed as the red cursor faded from the sonar screen. Rivetti shifted his glance from this schematic to the adjoining console's broadband waterfall display. Even though the noisy winch had been silenced, he knew that the damage had been done. And he really wasn't all that surprised when a dreaded flutter appeared on the display, indicating the presence of a submerged contact in the waters almost due west of them.

"Conn, sonar. Sierra two-eight is back. Bearing two-four-one!" shouted Rivetti into the overhead microphone.

"Holy shit, Sup!" interjected the sonarman monitoring the narrowband processor. "I'm picking up a launch transient from Sierra two-eight!"

Rivetti confirmed his terrifying observation with a single, swift glance at the narrowband screen, and the next report he relayed to the control room was the one every sonarman in the fleet most feared delivering.

"Conn, sonar. Torpedo in the water! Bearing two-four-one!"

"I've got another launch transient, Sup! Bearing two-four-two!" exclaimed the terrified seaman assigned to the narrowband scan.

"Conn, sonar. Second torpedo in the water, Sir! Bearing two-four-two!"

Inside the control room, Ramsey reacted to his lead sonarman's report with a firm forcefulness developed after decades' worth of endless drills and war games.

"All ahead flank!" he ordered. "Left full rudder!"

As the COB passed his command on to the helmsmen, Ramsey next addressed Lieutenant Linkletter, who, as TSO, stood to the captain's right, in front of the fire control console.

"TSO, launch the five-inch evasion device! Launch countermeasures!"

Then over the 1MC, Ramsey added, "Rig ship for collision!"

"Countermeasures away!" informed the TSO, in reference to the series of grinding decoys that had just been released from their amidships launch tubes.

"Conn, sonar," broke Rivetti's concerned voice over the PA. "Torpedoes are at three thousand yards and closing, sir."

"COB!" shouted Ramsey in response to this. "I want that flank speed, and I want it now!"

Ramsey was forced to reach up and grab an overhead handhold as the *Alabama* rolled over hard on its left side. Much like a high-performance jet fighter in the midst of a dogfight, the sub's rudder bit into the surrounding sea and the vessel turned hard aport in response.

"Maneuvering is answering to flank bell, Captain," reported the COB, who was kept in place by a seat belt. "Twenty-one knots . . . twenty-two . . . twenty-three . . ."

The digital knot indicator continued to display a steady increase in forward speed. Yet a vessel the size of the *Alabama* displaced well over 18,750 tons of seawater, and speed was not one of its design's strong points.

"Conn, sonar. Torpedoes are range-gaiting! Range is down to one-five-zero-zero yards and rapidly closing. Their active sonars appear to have a firm lock on us, sir!"

"Twenty-seven knots," reported the COB, an undeniable urgency to his tone.

"Conn, sonar. One thousand yards and closing fast!" Rivetti warned.

"Sound collision alarm!" ordered Ramsey.

As this wavering electronic alarm filled the ship with the dreaded sound, Hunter debated whether or not it was time for him to leave his post in the radio room. He had been readily able to follow the entire attack sequence over the public address system. Though there was little he could do to alter the inevitable outcome, he knew that his rightful place was at his captain's side. Yet before he could act on this impulse, Russell Vossler's voice redirected his thoughts.

"It looks like we're receiving a radio message from the VLF buoy!"

Having momentarily forgotten about the buoy's continued deployment, Hunter scanned the first line of the incoming message. What he saw on the glowing monitor screen caused his pulse to quicken, and he spoke forcefully into the intercom.

"Conn, radio. We're receiving an Emergency Action Message over the VLF buoy. Recommend Alert One!"

Inside the *Alabama*'s control room, Ramsey all but ignored his XO's report. He had more pressing concerns at the moment, his first priority being to save his endangered ship.

"TSO, launch another five-inch evasion device!" he ordered. "And I want a full spread of countermeasures in the water."

Returning his attention to the helm, Ramsey

added, "COB, shift your rudder to right full!"

Responding as quickly as if Ramsey had been at the helm himself, the helmsman turned his steering yoke hard to the right. The boat's rudder reversed itself, and the lumbering submarine turned over on its starboard side.

"Countermeasures away!" the TSO reported.

"I'm showing thirty-seven knots, Captain," observed COB. "Come on, *'Bama*! You can do it. Go baby, go!"

The COB's spirited urgings were overridden by the voice of Danny Rivetti. "Conn, sonar. Lead torpedo has taken the bait, sir. It's going after the decoy!"

This optimistic update however, was cut off by a deafening, gut-wrenching explosion, as the second torpedo detonated above the *Alabama*'s port bow. Immediately obliterated by the blast was the vessel's towed array radio cable, with the VLF buoy at its end.

Battered in the explosion's roiling vortex, the huge Trident submarine was tossed to and fro like a child's toy. Inside the warship, pipes burst, electrical circuits shorted out, and men were thrown to the deck—all as a result of this opening shot of the apocalypse.

Frank Ramsey knew from the mere fact that he had managed to remain on his feet that the explosion hadn't been a fatal one. Even though the control room's main lights had shorted out, and the hushed compartment was now lit with emergency battle lanterns, he addressed the 1MC, "All stations, report damage!"

From the diving control station, the COB checked in first. "Helm remains responsive, Captain. Reactor remains on-line, with maneuvering answering to all ahead standard."

Ever thankful that their vital power plant was intact, Ramsey listened as the boat's various departments began reporting in. The torpedo room appeared to have taken the brunt of the concussion. Two tubes sustained damage, and three torpedomen were injured. Throughout the rest of the ship the crew was battling several minor floods, all of which were brought under control by the time the control room's lights finally flickered back on.

Inside the adjoining radio room, Hunter delayed reporting until he and Zimmer had attended to a bloody gash that Russell Vossler had suffered above his right eye. Zimmer applied a cotton compress from the first aid kit to his assistant's cut, allowing Hunter to call in the tardy damage control report.

"Conn, radio. We need a corpsman in here! All communications systems are down, with what appears to be a total platform kill. Will commence troubleshooting at once, Captain."

Hunter returned his attention to their wounded shipmate. He used a clean compress to wipe off the blood that continued to stain Vossler's face. Surely the wound would need stitches, and Hunter breathed a sigh of relief as the corpsman finally arrived and took over.

That left Hunter and Zimmer free to survey the exact extent of the damages to their ability to receive and broadcast radio transmissions. Zimmer confirmed the fact that they had indeed suffered a total platform kill. It was as he was determining the possibility of getting the system back on-line that Hunter remembered the EAM that they had been receiving just before the blast occurred.

Hunter found the Emergency Action Message in the printer. He tore it off and quickly read it.

XREEBABA . . . . . . EMERGENCY ACTION MESSAGE (300)

FROM: NATIONAL MILITARY COMMAND CENTER
TO: USS ALABAMA (SSBN 731)
SUBJECT: NUCLEAR MISSILE LAUNCH.
SINGLE INTEGRATED . . .

"Oh, God, no!" exclaimed Hunter upon realizing that the message appeared to have been interrupted in mid-transmission by the attack. "Lieutenant Zimmer, is this all of the EAM that we got?"

Zimmer checked the computer and nodded that it was. "I'm afraid that's the extent of it, sir."

Hunter grimaced. With the partial EAM in hand, he proceeded into the control room to share it with the captain.

With each passing second, Ramsey's confidence in the *Alabama*'s ability to fulfil its primary mission increased. The sub's missile room had sustained a minimum amount of damage, allowing the countdown to resume with only the most minor of delays.

"Estimated time to 1SQ?" he asked Lieutenant Ince over the intercom.

"Estimated time to 1SQ, eight minutes, thirty seconds, sir," Weps replied.

Satisfied with this report, Ramsey's next intercom query was directed to Danny Rivetti. "Sonar, conn. What's the status of that Red bastard who took that potshot at us?"

"Conn, sonar. All sensors show that we've lost them, Captain."

"Keep looking for them, Rivetti," directed Ramsey. "One thing you can count on is that he's up there somewhere, looking for us."

To the COB and the rest of the diving control party, Ramsey spoke directly. "All right, gentlemen. Let's get on with it. All ahead one-third. Steady as you go. Make your depth one-five-zero feet, up real slow and silent to launch depth.''

"All ahead one-third. Steady on three-four-two. Make my depth one-five-zero feet, up slow and silent. Aye, sir," the COB repeated.

There was a self-satisfied sparkle in Ramsey's eyes as he watched the helmsmen pull back on their steering yokes. By the grace of God, they had prevailed, and now no force on earth could stop them from carrying out their all-important mission.

"Captain, I have the EAM that we were in the process of receiving immediately before that torpedo detonated," Hunter shouted from the accessway leading to the radio room.

"Let's see it," Ramsey replied with a minimum of enthusiasm.

Hunter handed him the dispatch, and Ramsey quickly scanned it.

"There's absolutely nothing of value on this thing," protested Ramsey, handing the message back to his XO.

"It got cut off during the attack, sir," explained Hunter.

"Then it's meaningless," he retorted.

"Sir, I beg to differ with you," dared Hunter. "This is a properly formatted EAM pertaining to nuclear missile launch."

Ramsey adamantly shook his head that such wasn't the case. "No, Mr. Hunter. That is a message fragment, and it doesn't mean a damn thing!"

"That's because of the attack, sir. This message could have contained any number of things. Captain, it could be a message to abort the launch!"

"Mr. Hunter," shot back Ramsey, his resolve firm, "did you ever think that this could be nothing more than a fake Russian transmission?''

Hunter took a deep breath and proceeded to express himself as clearly and precisely as possible. ''Which is why we must take the time to confirm, sir. All I'm asking for is the time to get our radio gear back on-line.''

''Mr. Hunter,'' said the captain, calm but stern, ''we have fully authenticated orders in hand. And those orders are to make a preemptive launch. Every second we lose increases the chance that by the time our missiles arrive, their silos could be empty, because they've flown their birds and struck us first. You know as well as I do that any launch order received without authentication is no order at all!''

''But, sir. National . . .''

Ramsey cut Hunter in mid-sentence. ''No ifs, ands, or buts, Mr. Hunter. That is our number one rule. That rule is the basis for the scenario that we've trained on time and time again. It's a rule that we follow without exception.''

''Sir, the National Military Command Center knows what sector we're operating in. They've got satellites looking down here, to see if our Tridents are aloft. And if they're not, they'll give our orders to somebody else. That's why we maintain more than one ballistic missile–carrying submarine. It's what they call redundancy!''

''I know all about redundancy, Mr. Hunter.''

''Then you understand that it's all part of our global strategy,'' urged Hunter. ''We have backup. That's the whole concept! Our duty is not to launch until we can confirm!''

Ramsey paused a moment to formulate his response. "Mr. Hunter, you presume that we have other submarines out there, ready to launch. As captain, I must assume that these submarines could have been taken out by the other Akulas. We can play these war games all night. But I don't have the luxury of your presumptions."

"But, sir—" protested Hunter.

Ramsey stopped him in his tracks. "Mr. Hunter, we have rules that are not open to interpretation, personal intuition, gut feelings, hairs on the back of your neck, or little devils or angels sitting on your shoulders.

"We are all very aware what our orders are, and what these orders mean. For they have come down from our commander-in-chief, and they contain no ambiguity."

Hunter was still not buying it, and he prepared to further argue his point. "Captain . . ."

"Mr. Hunter!" Ramsey shouted, having heard enough. "I have made the decision. I am captain of this boat. So shut the fuck up!"

With this crude invective, all eyes in the control room turned toward Ramsey. The captain ignored this attention with a casual shrug and redirected his attention to the coordinates on the launch order that he held in his hands.

"Weapons, conn," he said into the intercom, "shift targeting to target package SLBM six-four-seven-four-one-slash-two. This is the captain."

Ramsey handed the microphone to Hunter. Proper weapons release protocol demanded that the XO repeat these new coordinates as he had the previous launch orders. But in this instance, Hunter wouldn't budge.

"Captain," he said softly, "I cannot concur."

Dead silence followed his succinct reply. No one even moved, except for the COB, who left his post as diving officer and joined the two senior officers beside the missile indicator panel.

"Repeat my command, Mr. Hunter!" Ramsey ordered.

"Sir," said Hunter in a bare whisper, "we do not know what this last EAM said. Our target package could have even changed."

Quick to mimic the XO's cool demeanor, Ramsey readdressed him. "You will repeat this order or I shall find someone who will."

Hunter stubbornly held his ground. "Sir, I can't."

"You are relieved of your position!" snapped Ramsey. "COB, remove him from control. And get Lieutenant Zimmer in here, now!"

Undeterred by this threat, Hunter summoned the nerve to take his protest one step farther. "Captain, sir, I do not concur. And I do not recognize your authority to relieve me. Under navy regulations . . ."

"Arrest this man!" commanded Ramsey to the COB. "And get him out of my sight!"

The COB took a tentative step forward, and Hunter quickly tried to make his case one last time.

"Captain, under operating procedures governing the release of nuclear weapons, we can only launch our missiles if both you and I agree. This is not a formality, sir. This is expressly why your command must be repeated! It requires my assent. And I do not give it!"

Hunter's persuasive argument caused the COB

to freeze in midstep, unsure about what to do next. Ramsey noted the senior enlisted man's inaction, and he appeared both stunned and somewhat confused.

"COB, what in the hell are you waiting for? Arrest this man, and call in Lieutenant Zimmer!"

Hunter decided that now was the time to take the final step, and he held up the interrupted EAM and played his trump card. "And further, sir. If you continue upon this course and insist upon a missile launch, without first confirming this message, I will be forced—backed by the rules of precedence, authority, and command, sections zero-eight-one-five and zero-eight-six-seven, navy regulations—to relieve you of command."

"You son of a bitch!" cursed Ramsey. "Chief of the Boat, as captain and commanding officer of the USS *Alabama*, I order you to place the XO under arrest on the charge of mutiny!"

There was dead silence in the control room as the dreaded implication of the captain's last word sank in. To emphasize his point, Ramsey repeated it.

"I will say again. COB, I order you to place the XO under arrest on the charge of mutiny!"

All eyes turned to the COB. Torn by his personal loyalty to the captain, and his knowledge of naval law, the *Alabama*'s senior enlisted man was caught in a no-win dilemma that none of his shipmates envied.

"For God's sake, COB!" appealed Ramsey, with the sincerity of one friend to the other.

"Captain, sir," said the COB, after carefully weighing the facts and doing his best to ignore his emotions. "The XO is right. We can't launch unless he concurs."

Hardly believing what he was hearing, Ramsey picked up the authenticated EAM and began reading from it. "To: USS *Alabama*. Rebel-controlled missiles being fueled. Launch codes compromised. Dissidents threaten launch at Continental United States. Set DEFCON Two! IMMEDIATE LAUNCH TEN TRIDENT MISSILE SORTIES." Looking up to speak directly to the COB, he pleaded passionately. "Their missiles are being fueled. We don't have time to fuck around!"

"Sir," said Hunter, "until you have had a chance to think about this second EAM, that could have very well countermanded our original orders . . ."

"I don't have to think about it!" interrupted Ramsey.

"Then, sir," continued Hunter, almost apologetically, "I must relieve you as commanding officer of this ship. COB, please escort the captain to his stateroom. I am assuming command."

Ramsey looked at Hunter and bitterly countered. "You are not assuming anything!"

"Chief of the Boat, Captain Ramsey is under arrest. Lock him in his stateroom!"

Ignoring the XO, the COB focused his attention solely on Ramsey. "Captain," he pleaded. "Please . . ."

"Now, COB!" Hunter demanded, a new edge of authority to his tone.

"Aye, sir," said the COB, who unenthusiastically spoke to the two armed enlisted men who materialized out of the control room's shadows. "Take the captain below."

With the guards now at his side, Ramsey held eye contact with Hunter for one last flurry. "Mr. Hunter, you are way out of your league. You are not yet ready to make the tough decisions. You'll see."

In a final admission of defeat, Ramsey removed the lanyard holding the missile firing key from his neck and disgustedly threw it at Hunter. After a final look at the COB, Ramsey stormed out of the forward accessway with the two guards close on his heels.

There could be no hiding the looks of stunned disbelief that each member of the control team shared. Hunter squared his shoulders and bravely addressed them.

"If anyone disagrees with what I have done, feel free to relieve yourself of duty now."

Not a man moved, and Hunter looked at the COB, while reaching up for the 1MC to inform the crew.

"This is the XO. I have assumed command of this ship. Under authority granted to me by navy regulations, I've relieved Captain Ramsey of his duties for acting in contravention of the rules and regulations regarding the release of nuclear weapons.

"My intentions are to delay the missile launch, maintaining our current state of readiness, pending confirmation of an Emergency Action Message that was prematurely cut off as a result of the torpedo attack. You are to remain at battle stations missile. That is all."

Hunter switched off the intercom and looked at the COB, quietly saying, "Thanks."

"Fuck you," said COB, just as quietly. "And just to set the record straight, I'm not on your side, Hunter. You could be wrong. But wrong or right, the captain can't just replace you at will. That was completely improper on his part. That's why I did what I did, by the book."

"I thank you anyway," said Hunter. "Your father would be proud of you."

"What the hell is that supposed to mean?" the COB asked, totally perplexed by this off-the-wall remark.

"Have you already forgotten?" replied Hunter, fighting the urge to smile. "Right is right, and wrong's for nobody."

The source of the familiar adage hit home, and the COB's estimation of Hunter instantly went up a grudging notch. Prepared to help his new CO anyway he could, the COB returned to the diving console as Hunter initiated his new command with his first operational order.

"Bring the ship up to periscope depth, maintaining a state of ultra quiet. Remember, that Akula is still up there somewhere."

Then, into the intercom, he added. "Radio, conn. Mr. Zimmer, we need that radio system up and running, ASAP!"

"Conn, radio," replied Zimmer, the tension in his voice obvious. "We're tryin' our best, sir. But with this system crashed, and that VLF radio buoy severed, I'm afraid it just might take more than we've got."

Not the answer that he wanted to hear, Hunter

sighed heavily. Already the vast responsibility of command was weighing him down, as he was forced to make his concerns the same as those of his ship.

Danny Rivetti knew that there could be no worse
time to encounter a noisy pod of whales than the
present. Yet this very event occurred, shortly after
the deafening rumble of the exploding torpedo
faded from their hydrophone's transducers. The
whales had been with them ever since, filling the
depths with their wide-ranging, boisterous cries,
and making it that much more difficult to pick up
the signature of the hostile Akula.

Because their very lives were on the line, Danny
personally took over the monitoring of the narrowband sonar console. With headphones tightly
cupped over his ears, and his gaze locked on the
CRT screen, his difficult task was to scan the limited frequency range over which the Akula would
be audible. Since the whales' melodious aria also
ranged into this same frequency, he had to concentrate on picking out which sounds were man-made
and which were cetacean.

As he did his best to filter out the deep, bass
whale bellow that currently filled his headphones,
Rivetti thought about the CD that he had been listening to recently. In any other circumstances, he

would have considered monitoring a pod of singing whales a welcome change of pace. During previous watches, whales had given him hours of fascinating entertainment, becoming companions with whom he whiled away the hours of many a lonely watch. In fact, Danny hoped to record such songs one day, and after mixing them with a jazz-fusion sound track, produce an album that he planned to call "Cry of the Deep." Unfortunately, for the first time in his relatively short naval career, he didn't even know if he'd live to see that day come.

They had miraculously survived the Akula's attack, with one torpedo drawn away by a decoy, and the other prematurely detonating above them. A last-minute impulse on Danny's part had his men switch off the volume gains of their headphones just as the warhead exploded. This saved their eardrums, and the damages in sonar were limited to the loss of their towed array unit and several spilled coffee cups. But the Akula was still out there somewhere.

And the arrival of real launch orders meant political events topside had spiraled so out of control, his government was willing to strike first and initiate World War III.

But the Akula's attack and their launch, these he could understand. If he hadn't ever given them much chance of occurring, he had trained for years to respond perfectly in the event they did. The mutiny, however, was an entirely different matter.

Though the details of the mutiny were sketchy, from what he could gather, it revolved around a direct confrontation between Captain Ramsey and Lieutenant Commander Hunter regarding the legit-

imacy of their launch orders. For the XO actually
to go to the extreme of assuming command meant
that his doubts must have had a good degree of
substantiation. Danny couldn't help but like Hunter. But he genuinely respected Captain Ramsey as
well, and this was where it got confusing.

Upon hearing Hunter's announcement that he
was relieving Captain Ramsey of his duties, Danny
and the three members of his watch team became
immersed in a furious debate. Two of his shipmates
wanted to go immediately to Captain Ramsey and
offer their support. Danny did his best to calm them
down. He insisted that the whole mess was none
of their business, and if they knew what was good
for them, they'd let the officers deal with it. Mean-
while, they had a much more important task to focus on—retagging the enemy submarine that had
almost blown them away!

Somewhere outside their hull, one particular
whale was in the midst of a remarkably complex
song. It was characterized by a long drawn-out series of bull-like bellows, followed by a burst of
sonorous, hollow clicks.

The *Alabama* was currently ascending, on its
way to periscope depth. Because the towed array
was inoperable, Danny decided to shift his focus to
the hydrophones nearest the boat's stern. The deep
cries of the bellowing whale could still be heard
there, and he addressed the keyboard in an effort
to filter out the persistent biologic.

It was as he scanned the lowest portion of the
audible hertz range, in that part of the ocean almost
directly behind them, that the barest of aberrations
broke the solid white line of the narrowband's wa-

terfall display. He turned up his headphones to full volume, and, as he closed his eyes to concentrate, the briefest of faint pulses could be heard. It faded as quickly as it had appeared, and Danny knew that its source could be as diverse as a mere anomaly, an unspecified biologic, or even a by-product of one of the whales.

It was the unnatural throbbing nature of the contact that caused him to discount those possibilities. Guided more by intuition than raw fact, he allowed his gut to guide him, and he reached out tentatively for the nearest intercom handset.

"Conn, sonar," broke the anxious voice of Danny Rivetti over the control room's PA speaker. "We have a submerged contact. Bearing zero-four-five. Classify Sierra two-nine, possible hostile submarine."

Hunter had been standing behind the COB, intently studying the diving control station's rapidly decreasing digital depth guage, as this report arrived. Fully aware of its possible consequences, he grabbed the nearest intercom handset.

"Sonar, conn. Mr. Rivetti, is it the Akula?"

"Conn, sonar," replied Rivetti hesitantly. "Sir, though I really can't be one hundred percent positive, Sierra two-nine's aspect is definitely suspicious."

Hunter ingested the wavering response and considered its source. From what he had already seen of the chief sonarman's work, Petty Officer Rivetti appeared to be a most-competent technician. Just as much of an artist as a scientist, a successful sonarman combined a thorough knowledge of his equipment with an artist's instinctive ability to see beyond the obvious. He was the eyes and ears of the ship, whose abilities alone could mean the difference between life and death. Hunter thus had no other alternative but to trust Rivetti in this instance.

"All stop!" he firmly ordered. "Prepare for snap shot, tubes two and four. COB, bring us ten up on the bow. If Sierra two-nine is indeed our Akula, I want to be ready to take it out at the least provocation."

The all stop maneuver caused the *Alabama* to lose its forward momentum. The ten-degree up angle forced the sub's stern to drop, so that its bow-mounted torpedo tubes now had a clear line of fire at any target that threatened from above.

With the torpedo tubes flooded and their doors open, the *Alabama* was fully ready to defend itself. And that was just what it was forced to do when Sierra two-nine suddenly became fully alive on the *Alabama*'s sonar screens.

"Conn, sonar. I'm picking up definite screw noises on Sierra two-nine. Relative rough range six hundred yards on bearing zero-four-eight."

Noting the close range, Hunter fought the impulse to fire their torpedoes immediately. He urgently pondered the options, which narrowed considerably as a result of the next sonar update.

"Conn, sonar. Torpedoes in the water, sir! Bearings zero-four-eight and zero-five-zero."

"Shit!" cursed Hunter, who allowed his extensive training to take over. "Launch port countermeasures! All ahead full! Zero bubble, left full rudder! Rig ship for collision."

The collision alarm began wailing in the background. Hunter reached up to grab on to an overhead handhold as the *Alabama* lurched forward and began a tight turn.

"XO, countermeasures are away!" shouted Lieutenant Linkletter from the fire control console. "Shouldn't we fire back? Torpedoes are ready, sir."

Hunter answered without diverting his glance from the slowly rising knot indicator. "We're too close. Our weapons won't have time to arm. COB, all ahead flank. Give me max speed, now!"

As the COB passed this urgent request on to maneuvering, Hunter activated the intercom.

"Sonar, conn. Mr. Rivetti, let me know the instant that our range to target opens to one thousand yards."

Hunter dropped the microphone, and turned toward fire control. "TSO, you be ready for that snap shot the instant we pass the one-thousand-yard threshold!"

"Aye, sir," returned Linkletter. "Tubes two and four ready to fire."

"Conn, sonar. Torpedoes continue their approach. Range one-five-zero yards and closing fast."

Hunter listened to the dismal news and peered up to the ceiling to quietly petition the seas outside their hull. "Come on, countermeasures, do your thing!"

The high-pitched, range-gaiting ping of the Akula's torpedoes seemingly answered Hunter's request, and he regripped his handhold in anticipation of the explosion he feared would soon befall them. Seconds were like minutes; a minute, an hour. Hunter was barely aware of the perspiration gathering on his forehead or the mad pounding of his pulse. Instead his thoughts were focused on the peculiar fact that the persistent pinging of the Russian torpedoes seemed to be lessening in volume. This fact was confirmed by the excited voice of Danny Rivetti.

"Conn, sonar. The fuckers missed us, sir! The torpedoes were too close to arm and passed astern! Range to Akula, nine-five-zero yards and opening fast."

Ignoring the unorthodox terminology used in this sonar update, Hunter began silently counting off the seconds. "TSO, go to manual on the arming mechanisms, tubes two and four," he instructed Linkletter. "Snap shot, two and four!"

"Snap shot, two and four!" the TSO repeated, while hitting two red buttons on the fire control panel. "Tubes fired electrically, sir."

A barely noticeable lurch signaled the release of the weapons. Hunter again peered upward, visualizing the two Mk-48 torpedoes as they shot out of their portside tubes. When their engines ignited, they would arc upward toward the Russian sub above, which would most likely respond with a desperate release of its own countermeasures.

To gauge this action properly, Hunter again contacted Danny Rivetti. "Sonar, conn. Give me exact ranging and speed."

"Range three hundred yards at fifty knots, sir," Rivetti alertly answered.

"Rig ship for impact," Hunter warned, anticipating a successful torpedo hit on their part. "Zero bubble. Steady course two-three-one."

"Aye, sir. Zero bubble, course two-three-one," repeated the COB.

"One hundred yards, fifty-five knots," added Rivetti over the PA. "Approaching seventy-five yards, sir. Weapons ready for arming!"

"Arm torpedoes two and four, now!" Hunter ordered.

The TSO instantly flicked a pair of red switches set on the top portion of his console. "Torpedoes are armed, sir!"

Once more, Hunter began counting off the seconds. The Akula would be picking up speed now, its crew sharing the same anxieties that the men of the *Alabama* had just experienced. But would the outcome be the same?

"Our torpedoes have just gone active!" Rivetti reported. "I show them firmly locked on target, sir!"

Hunter knew full well that this signaled the Akula's doom. Two hard heartbeats later, his realization was confirmed.

"Conn, sonar. Torpedoes have detonated," observed Rivetti, almost as an afterthought.

The arrival of the blast's aftershock verified his report. As the wall of turbulent seawater slammed into the *Alabama*, the sub rocked hard on its side. The lights flickered off, then on again, and as the hull stabilized, it was soon evident which submarine had prevailed.

"Conn, sonar. I'm picking up breaking-up sounds from the Akula, sir," said Rivetti, his tone somber, with an almost funereal heaviness. "It almost sounds like crackling popcorn, sir. That Akula's history."

With his words, a wave of cheers escaped the lips of the men in the control room. Hunter returned the COB's grin, and accepted a thumbs-up from the TSO. Yet any further celebration on their part was abruptly cut short by, of all things, the frantic voice of Danny Rivetti.

"Incoming torpedoes! Bearing zero-eight-six, zero-eight-eight. Range one-five-zero yards, and closing fast!"

"Jesus, it's those two fish from the Akula!" shouted Hunter. "Right full rudder, all ahead flank! Launch starboard countermeasures!"

His desperate orders were repeated and then executed. Hunter decided that the best place to escape the Russian torpedoes was in the depths of the sea.

"Take us down, COB! Full angle on the diving planes. Make your new depth twelve hundred feet!"

The planesmen pushed hard on their yokes, and the *Alabama* responded by sharply angling downward by the bow. Hunter's body jerked forward, and he had to regrasp the overhead handhold to keep from losing his footing and crashing into the forward bulkhead.

His worried glance constantly shifted back and forth between the depth gauge and the knot indicator. Just as the digital display passed 553 feet, an earsplitting pair of explosions broke the tense silence.

Hunter had little time to react to the blast as a powerful wave of turbulent seawater crashed into the sub's hull. Thrown to the deck by the sheer force of this collision, Hunter smacked into the edge of the diving control station and had the wind knocked out of his lungs. As he painfully fought to regain his breath, the overhead lights failed. The sickening sound of spraying water resounded through the vessel, and Hunter struggled to his knees just as the emergency battle lanterns popped on.

The red-tinted lights illuminated a scene of utter devastation. Except for the COB and the two helmsman, who were held into their chairs by seat belts, every other member of the control room team had been upended. Alongside the fallen sailors, an assortment of debris littered the deck, most of which had originated at the overturned navigation plot.

The collision alarm wavered monotonously in the distance. Hunter struggled to his feet, and while gripping the back edge of the COB's chair, felt the powerful force of inertia pulling his body forward. He didn't need to look at the rapidly falling numbers of the depth gauge to know that they were in the midst of a spiraling dive to oblivion.

"How does she answer, COB?" Hunter worriedly asked.

COB dejectedly shook his head. "It's no good, sir. We've lost all propulsion, and we're goin' down!"

Not about to give up without a fight, Hunter grabbed a sound-powered telephone. "All stations, I need damage control reports!"

The first arrived from the sub's lowest deck. "Control, this is Chief Rono in the bilge bay. We have uncontrolled flooding! Request a damage control team. Need bandit kits, wedges, and lead, sir! And you'd better get 'em down here real quick!"

"Control, maneuvering," reported the next station to react. "Request damage control party, at once! Reactor has emergency scrammed!"

Similar reports began arriving from all over the ship, and Hunter did his best to direct the badly stretched damage control teams to the worst casualties first. Of course, all of their efforts would be in vain, if the *Alabama* couldn't be pulled out of its current dive, which the COB vocalized for all to hear.

"Nine-five-zero feet . . . Approaching one thousand feet. If we don't get propulsion, we're history."

"Chief Hunsicker, blow the ballast tanks, emergency blow!" Hunter ordered.

"Can't do, sir," informed the officer of the watch. "Forward ballast tank air pressure is zero."

With that avenue eliminated, Hunter resolutely changed his plan of attack. "Then it all depends on restoring propulsion and getting that damn flooding in the bilge bay stopped!"

It was in the middle of all this chaos that the *Alabama*'s supply officer fought his way up to the boat's third level stairwell. Because of the sharp downward angle of the deck, gravity made his climb that much more difficult. But Chop stubbornly persisted, and he breathlessly completed his short transit, now finding himself directly opposite the officers' study, in the forward compartment, second level.

From here he turned to his right and followed the sloping passageway to the closed door of the captain's stateroom. Two sentries, wearing holstered .45 caliber pistols, stood on each side of the door. Chop recognized both of them as being machinist mates second class. Neither one of them looked very happy with his current duty, their concerned expressions displaying more fear than anything else.

"I've got to talk to the captain!" greeted Chop firmly.

"I'm sorry, Lieutenant Dougherty, sir," replied the tallest of the two enlisted men. "The XO ordered us to . . ."

"Screw the XO," Chop interrupted. "Don't you realize what's coming down? The ship has been seriously hit, and I want to speak to my captain!"

Daring either of the sailors to further block his way, Chop removed a master key from his pocket and unlocked the door. He entered swiftly, shut the door behind him, and found Ramsey contentedly sitting at his desk. He had Bear in his lap, and had been busy reading the contents of a thick file folder.

"How bad is it, Mr. Dougherty?" asked Ramsey matter-of-factly.

Astounded by the captain's remarkable composure, Chop answered. "Bad, sir. There's serious flooding in the bilge, and a good deal of damage in the engine room. The reactor's scrammed, and engineering has lost all propulsion."

"I've been reading Mr. Hunter's personnel file," revealed Ramsey, completely heedless of Chop's somber damage control assessment. "It would appear the closest he's been to combat until now is a policy seminar."

The lights suddenly flickered. An exterior hull plate buckled loudly, and Bear's head shot up, concerned. While Ramsey calmed his pet with a gentle stroke of his hand, Chop revealed the reason for his visit.

"Give me an order, sir."

Expecting such a request, Ramsey readily fulfilled it. "Mr. Dougherty, as quietly as you can, get lieutenants Zimmer and Westerguard."

"What about Linkletter?" questioned Chop.

Ramsey shook his head. "The TSO is inside control. You won't be able to talk to him. But you can get to Weps. We gotta have Weps, he's the key. So you get me those men, and a small security force. Then come and get me. Don't get overzealous and try to recruit the whole ship. We'll lead from the top on down."

"Aye, sir," said Chop with enthusiasm. "I'm on my way!"

A struggle of a much different kind was taking place two decks below, in the *Alabama*'s bilge bay. In the cramped drainage space beneath the torpedo room, a torrent of frigid water was pouring into the ship from a fractured seawater ballast pipe. Bravely fighting this flood, knee deep in the ever-rising brine, were Chief Howard Rono and seamen Barnes and Lawson.

It was the sounding of battle stations that had originally called Chief Rono to this section of the ship from his normal watch in the galley. As the senior enlisted man present, Rono called the shots, while also taking the brunt of the soaking.

"Barnes, open the after main drain suction!" he shouted over the deafening roar of pouring water.

"I'm startin' the drain pump, Chief," informed Seaman Lawson.

The pump activated with a growl, and Lawson sloshed his way across the flooded compartment to help Rono repair the burst pipe. Together they struggled to cover the fracture with a strongback. It took a great deal of effort to fit the curved metallic cylinder around the broken section, and they had to briefly halt their efforts when a bolt blew out of the bulkhead and shot overhead, just missing them.

Seaman Barnes arrived with several steel restraining bands in tow. It took all three of them to wrap the bands around the strongback, and it was Rono who hammered down the dog clips to keep the bands in place.

Instead of pouring out in a torrent, the water sprayed wildly in all directions. The volume was greatly reduced, though, and it was a very relieved Chief Rono who spoke into the sound-powered telephone to relay their success.

"Control, bilge bay. Flooding has slowed! We have it under control, sir!"

Now finding himself with one less problem to be concerned with, Hunter was able to focus fully on the number one danger facing them.

"One-two-five-zero feet, sir," reported the COB, a noticeable tenseness in his voice. "Approaching thirteen hundred feet."

"Sir," whispered the young helmsman seated to the COB's left. "Aren't we gettin' close to the 'Bama's crush depth?"

The COB reached out and gently massaged the tense muscles of the helmsman's neck. "Easy does it, son. The folks at EB designed our hull to withstand a lot more pressure than the specs called for.

As far as I know, since this is as deep as a Trident has ever gone, God only knows how much water pressure we'll really be able to withstand.''

Back inside the bilge bay, Chief Rono and his men worked on securing a strongback to a section of overhead piping that was just starting to show signs of leaking. Their earlier repair continued to hold, and with the invaluable assistance of the growling drain pump, the water level was consistently dropping, now hitting the men at mid-thigh.

"We just gotta strap on this last strongback, and our work down here will be finished," observed Rono as he struggled to hold the metallic cover plate over the leak, while his assistants installed the restraining straps.

The crushing sound of an exterior deck plate buckling outside underscored his comment, causing Seaman Barnes to remark worriedly, "Is plugging this leak really gonna make a difference, Chief? The *'Bama*'s going down regardless of our work here."

"Hold your tongue, boy!" castigated Rono. "This ole lady's got plenty of fight left in her, and talk like that won't be tolerated."

Satisfied that he had set the record straight, Rono looked on as Barnes and Lawson solidified the hold of the restraining bandit straps with a series of dog clips. He was able to let go of the strongback, and a satisfied grin turned the corners of his mouth upon seeing that the leak had all but stopped.

"Good work," he said, doing his best to ignore the hull's persistent groaning as the water pressure squeezed it ever more intensely.

"Now, let's get the hell out of here. As promised, the moment the *'Bama*'s out of harm's way, it's steaks, pizza, and ice cream for the rest of the patrol, and screw the cholesterol!''

The steep, downward slope of the deck and the thigh-level water made their transit to the open hatchway difficult. The constantly buckling deck plates motivated them onward, with Rono leading the way and Barnes and Lawson close behind.

A mere ten feet from the hatch, Rono briefly halted and turned around for a final inspection of their repair work. The bilge bay's main lights remained inoperable, and he had to remove a portable battle lantern to properly illuminate the maze of overhead piping.

''God damn it!'' he cursed, upon spotting several dog clips on the nearest strongback that had somehow managed to pop open. ''Come on, guys. Our job's not done until we hammer down those clips!''

His men moaned in protest. But it only took a single menacing glance on Rono's part to inspire them to follow the head cook back into the partially flooded bilge.

It took both Rono and Barnes to clamp down the bandit strap with their outstretched hands. That left Lawson free to hammer down the dog-clip that would keep the strap in place permanently.

Lawson's first hammer blow failed to engage the clip. Once more he was forced to swing the hammer overhead, and this time when he struck the clip it sheared off.

In quick succession, the remaining portion of the dog clip broke off, the bandit strap whipped away, and the heavy metal strongback crashed down hard onto Lawson's head. A torrent of icy seawater poured out of the uncovered fracture with such velocity that Barnes lost his footing and fell down onto the flooded deck.

With Lawson immobilized against a rack of piping, blood gushing from his head wound, and Barnes no longer visible, his body submerged beneath several feet of seawater, Chief Howard Rono selflessly snapped into action. His first priority was to find Barnes and pull him up before he drowned. And it was with this goal in mind that he blindly dived beneath the frigid, blackened waters.

"Control, this is Ensign Moder at the bilge bay hatch. Flooding has recommenced in the bilge, sir. Chief Rono and his two-man damage control party are trapped inside!"

Hunter listened to the frantic report from his command perch in the control room. The *Alabama*'s uncontrolled descent had yet to be stemmed, and the flooding could very well be the casualty that would seal their doom.

"Passing sixteen hundred feet, sir," reported the COB from the diving control station. "Sir," he urgently added, "if we don't seal the bilge bay, we will flood the entire forward compartment and lose the ship."

Hunter was fully aware of that fact. Yet he was still hesitant to give the order that would cost three brave men their lives.

"Control, this is Ensign Moder. The flooding has intensified! The chief and his men are trapped in the after portion of the bay, and I seriously doubt that we'll be able to reach them before the water level compromises the hatch."

That was all Hunter had to hear to prompt him to issue the order that every commanding officer most feared. "Bilge bay, conn. Seal the bay, Ensign Moder."

A strained moment of silence followed, and Hunter was forced to repeat his order. "I say again. Seal the bay, Ensign!"

This finally generated a response from the confused ensign, though not necessarily the one that Hunter wanted to hear. "But, sir. Chief Rono and his men will drown . . ."

"Ensign Moder!" Hunter forcefully shouted into the microphone. "You have your orders. Seal that goddamn bay now, before we all go down!"

Hunter was barely aware of the harsh stares from his fellow shipmates in control. He knew that he had just condemned three men to death. It was a decision that he'd have to live with for the rest of his life, however long that might be.

"Control, bilge bay," sounded Ensign Moder's somber voice over the PA. "Seawater hatch is sealed, sir."

"Very well, Ensign," whispered Hunter, most aware that the horrible deed had been done.

So deep was Hunter's remorse that he was hardly conscious of a sudden flutter of the control room's backup lights. From a distant place the COB's gruff voice informed him that they were passing seventeen hundred feet, a depth that no Trident had even gotten close to before. Death had once more paid the USS *Alabama* a visit, and Hunter could only pray that this would be the last of it.

Hunter was in the process of petitioning a God he was just then rediscovering when the main lights unexpectedly turned on. The relieved voice of the sub's chief engineer over the PA immediately followed.

"Conn, maneuvering. The reactor is back online. Turbine power has been restored. Ready to answer bells. Propulsion limit, ahead full."

His prayers seemingly answered, Hunter returned his attention to the diving control station. "All ahead full, COB. Twenty up."

"All ahead full, twenty-degree up angle, aye, sir," readily returned COB.

Hunter watched as the helmsmen yanked back on their yokes. Yet even with the engagement of the diving planes, the depth gauge continued to drop. All so slowly, the digital knot indicator began registering. This showed that the *Alabama*'s propeller had started to turn. But the question remained, was it too late?

"One-seven-five-zero feet," the COB announced tensely.

The hull popped and groaned. With each passing foot, the hull welds got that much closer to the breaking point.

When the depth gauge clicked past an unprecedented eighteen hundred feet, the COB couldn't resist whispering to Chief Hunsicker, his chief of the watch. "Hell, Hunsy. If we sink any farther, you can stick a fork in us. We're done!"

Hunter overhead his remark and he knew that the COB was right. They were well below a Trident's supposed crush depth, and Lord only knew what was keeping their hull from imploding.

"One-eight-two-five feet," said the COB, who

suddenly sat forward upon spotting a change in their angle of descent. "It's the bubble!" he joyously exclaimed. "We're pulling out of our dive! Holding at one-eight-two-five feet and rising!"

13

As the USS *Alabama* slowly emerged out of the unforgiving black depths that had almost swallowed it, the vessel's weapons officer began an extensive damage control check of the missile compartment. With clipboard in hand, Weps began his inspection in the mid-level compartment. He was particularly concerned with any damage that might have affected the launch system's ability to pressurize properly. Each of the twenty-four missile tubes had a primary readout gauge that could only be accessed in the mid-level. A careful inspection of each of these gauges was Weps' current priority.

He was well into this task, and so absorbed in his work that he was caught by surprise by the unexpected arrival of three of his shipmates. They appeared at his side while he was in the midst of recording the psi level of tube number seven, and it was Roy Zimmer's voice that announced their arrival.

"Hey, Weps, did the launch system survive?"

He looked up from his clipboard and replied while scanning the faces of lieutenants Zimmer,

Dougherty, and Westerguard. "So far, so good. I
don't suppose that you're here to give me a hand
with my damage control checklist?"

The boat's communications officer got right
down to business. "That we aren't, Weps. We're
here in regard to the mutiny. Speaking for myself,
I will not let the XO get away with it!"

"I agree," said Chop. "I've sailed with the captain for years, and now, because Hunter says so,
I'm supposed to be following him?"

Weps couldn't believe what he was hearing, and
he expressed himself frankly. "You are not supposed to merely follow the XO, Chop. You have
been ordered to. That's what this whole change of
command is all about. Proper orders, Mr. Dougherty. If they want us to launch, the XO will launch.
Hell, we'll blow them all to kingdom come! But
I'd rather go down myself, than get those orders
wrong."

Darik Westerguard calmly intervened. "Look,
our procedures are clear. In the absence of a con-
travening order, in a situation like this, you follow
the orders in hand."

Zimmer alertly chimed in. "You know how
many checks we go through to make sure a launch
order is authentic, Weps. The XO agreed himself!
And now he wants to throw them away?"

"Ah, he's lost his nerve," offered Chop.

"No way," countered Weps. "You forget, I personally know this guy."

Zimmer returned to his original argument.
"Look, Weps, the one thing that you can't deny is
that we've definitely been ordered to launch."

"Now, why in the world would they do that,"

interjected Westerguard, "if the Russians weren't gonna launch at us?"

Weps appeared slightly flustered and he put down his clipboard and replied, "But we still don't know that for sure, Darik. Don't you see? This isn't a matter of launch or don't launch. All Hunter wants is time to confirm that original EAM."

"But we don't have time for that, Peter!" Zimmer passionately observed. "Radchenko is fueling his birds. That, my friend, is a fact. And the Russians wouldn't go to all the trouble of prepping their ICBMs unless they intended to launch 'em."

This point momentarily stymied Weps. His convictions gradually weakening, he slowly scanned the faces of his fellow officers and decided it was time to hear how they intended to proceed.

"I'm almost afraid to ask, but what are you gonna do?"

Zimmer knew that they had him now, and he quickly spoke out. "Nothing, without you, Weps. You're a senior officer, a respected department head. The TSO's with Hunter . . ."

"And you have the keys to the small arms locker," blurted Westerguard. "All we wanna do is recruit a few more men and then open the arsenal."

"This is a mutiny, Peter," Zimmer reminded. "There's only two sides in a mutiny. The captain's asking for your help."

Weps found himself perplexed. Unable to come up with any further justification not to join his shipmates and unwilling to appear to be supporting the XO just because the two of them shared the same race, Weps reluctantly caved in.

"All right. I'm with you."

* * *

With a minimum of fanfare, the four conspirators fanned out through the ship, to recruit some additional manpower. Four willing enlisted men were subsequently selected and their next stop was the small arms locker.

Still not one hundred percent confident that he was doing the right thing, Weps unlocked the locker. An assortment of shotguns, M-16s, and semiautomatic pistols were stored there in secure racks. Chop and Zimmer distributed the weapons and ammunition, while Weps gave each of the enlisted men a bulletproof vest and a pair of handcuffs. Thus armed and ready for combat, they headed at once to the captain's stateroom.

Chop was in the point position. On his hand signal they halted in the passageway alongside the ship's office.

"There're two sentries still on watch outside the captain's stateroom," Chop informed them. "Let's go in quick and clean. We'll cuff 'em and then lock 'em in Ramsey's quarters after we free the skipper."

It was decided to let the four enlisted men lead the attack. They rushed in so swiftly that the two bored machinist mates who were standing guard were disarmed and handcuffed before they knew what hit them. Chop only had to put his finger to his lips to ensure their silence.

Weps relieved them of their keys and opened the locked door. He found the captain calmly seated at his desk smoking a cigar. Bear was peacefully snoozing at his feet, and Ramsey didn't appear the least bit surprised as Weps urgently greeted him.

"Come on, Captain. Let's go!"

Continuing to display a remarkable degree of casualness, Ramsey put down his cigar and stood. He made it a point to walk over to the mirror and adjust the fit of his crimson USS *Alabama* ball cap before joining Weps at the doorway.

"Thank you, Mr. Ince," he commented curtly.

"Aye, sir," replied Weps, his stomach tightening.

Ramsey stepped out into the passageway. He warmly smiled upon spotting Zimmer, Dougherty, Westerguard, and their four-man security detail standing there.

"Okay, gentlemen," he softly said. "Let's get on with it."

Inside the *Alabama*'s control room, a more relaxed, business-as-usual atmosphere was finally prevailing. Hunter stood on the periscope pedestal. From this centrally located position he clearly heard the COB's latest depth update.

"We're comin' up nice and easy. Three hundred feet."

"COB," instructed Hunter, "I want to proceed as silently as possible to periscope depth and reestablish communications as quickly as possible."

"Aye, sir," the COB replied, ever mindful of one all-important, missing detail. "But the radio, sir?"

Hunter crisply spoke into the intercom to address this concern. "Radio, conn. Mr. Zimmer, report!"

"Conn, radio," returned a tense voice over the PA. "Lieutenant Zimmer isn't here, sir."

"Radio, conn. What's the status of your repairs?" Hunter asked anyway.

"Conn, radio. All systems are still down, sir. The repair effort is continuing as best we can."

Hunter switched off the intercom and absently peered out at the instruments of the diving control station. With the radio still inoperable, there was absolutely no reason for Zimmer to be absent. Hunter's greatest fear was that the other officers would band together and challenge his right to assume command. Zimmer's absence could very well signal that just such a movement was presently under way, and Hunter knew he'd better plan for the worst.

"Lieutenant Linkletter, take the conn!" he ordered.

Before exiting the control room, Hunter stopped to have a discreet word with the COB. "Chief, I want you to send a man to track down Lieutenant Zimmer. And under the circumstances, I think you'd better have someone bring you a sidearm."

"Aye, sir," said the COB.

Hunter left by way of the forward passageway, and made a quick left-hand turn into sonar. Inside the dimly lit compartment, three technicians were hunched over their consoles, ignorant of his presence. Hunter looked on relieved as Danny Rivetti emerged from the adjoining storage closet. He silently beckoned the senior sonarman to join him beside the closed doorway.

"What's up, sir?" asked Rivetti innocently.

Hunter reached into his pants pocket and removed his key chain. "Mr. Rivetti, I'd like you to hold on to these keys for me."

Rivetti accepted the key chain, a puzzled expression filling his face. "Whatever for, sir?"

"Just hold them for me, sailor. You'll know the right time to return them," Hunter said with a cryptic wink.

Applying the same intuitive ability that made him such a successful sonarman, Danny sensed trouble in the offing. "Sir, is everything going to be all right? I mean, with the captain and all?"

"Son, if we can escape four separate torpedo salvos and a dive into depths that would have crushed lesser vessels, we'll see our way through this crisis as well. By the way, that was some damn fine work you did, anticipating that last attack. I owe you guys, big time. And when we get back home, the Snickers are on me!"

Rivetti smiled, and as he pocketed the keys, Hunter turned to exit. His next stop was at the radio room, which was situated directly opposite sonar. The stench of burnt wiring filled the air here. A pair of sailors were absorbed in the repairing of several stripped-apart consoles. Seeing that Lieutenant Zimmer wasn't one of them, Hunter asked who was in charge.

An enlisted man wearing a large butterfly bandage on his forehead looked up from his work. "I am, sir."

Hunter recognized him as being Petty Officer Second Class Russell Vossler, the sailor to whom he had applied first aid earlier. Vossler appeared to be a capable young man. Yet Hunter couldn't emphasize enough the vital importance of their current repair effort.

"How long is it gonna take you, Mr. Vossler?"

Vossler sheepishly shook his head. "I can't really say, sir."

''Do you know what's going on here?'' persisted Hunter.

''Yes, sir,'' Vossler replied.

Hunter nevertheless reminded him. ''If you don't get this system up, we could screw up so badly you cannot imagine.''

''Yes, sir. I know that, sir.''

''I doubt if you really do, sailor. Because it's much worse than whatever you're thinking. If we launch and we're not right, what's left of Russia is gonna launch at us. I'm talking about thousands of nuclear warheads here that will create a holocaust beyond imagination. There will be nothing left to go home to. Do you understand me?''

Vossler was clearly shaken, and he struggled to summon his words. ''Aye, sir.''

''This whole thing is about knowing, son. We have to know if the order to launch has been recalled or not. And it all depends on your fixing this radio. Get this system up and running, gentlemen!''

Certain that he got his point across, Hunter stormed out of the compartment. A short transit brought him back into the control room, where he quickly resumed command.

''I have the conn. COB, make your depth seven-five feet. Come to periscope depth.''

''Belay that order!'' broke a deep, authoritative voice from the aft accessway.

Hunter spun around to see who dared to countermand him. Entering the control room in quick succession were Captain Ramsey, lieutenants Zimmer, Dougherty, Westerguard, and Ince, and four heavily armed enlisted men. With weapons raised, they spread out to cover the entire compartment.

"If any of you officers or chiefs believe that you've been unjustly caught up in this," said Ramsey while stepping up onto the periscope pedestal, "stand behind me now."

This offer was met with dead silence, and not a soul moved. Impressed with this initial display of loyalty, Hunter watched as two ensigns left their posts at the navigation plot and joined Ramsey's forces. This left Lieutenant Linkletter, their navigator, an ensign assigned to the tactical systems watch, and Chief Hunsicker and the COB remaining on Hunter's side.

"Lock them in the officers' mess," directed Ramsey.

A tall, muscular, blond-haired sailor holding a .45 pistol stepped forward to take Hunter's arm and lead him away. Hunter recognized this mean-faced enlisted man as Seaman Bennefield, the fellow Danny Rivetti had been about to duke it out with down in crew's berthing. Not about to give Bennefield the satisfaction of touching him, Hunter yanked his arm away and turned to face the captain.

"Sir," he said in a bare whisper, "propulsion has been restored. The flooding has been contained. All communications systems are still inoperable."

In a final act of compliance, Hunter removed the lanyard holding the captain's missile firing key from around his neck. Ramsey readily grabbed it and spoke out in disgust.

"Take them away, and lock them up!"

To the officers on his side, Ramsey added, "Please return to your stations, and inform your men directly that the captain is in command. I have the conn!"

As Hunter was escorted out the forward accessway, he passed by Peter Ince. Weps tried hard to avoid his glance and Hunter left him with a bitter last word.

"Thanks."

The same disappointment that Hunter felt toward Weps was shared by Frank Ramsey, as the COB passed by him. Another old friendship had bitten the dust, and this time it was Ramsey who had the last word.

"You, COB. Of all the people!"

With his head bowed in shame, the COB was led out of the compartment. The last of the mutineers were now gone, and Ramsey was quick to assume total control.

"Mr. Ince, return to missile control. Mr. Zimmer, you are to stay with me."

Weps took off for the aft hatchway. With his exit, all eyes were on Ramsey as he stepped up to the captain's missile indicator panel and addressed the crew over the 1MC.

"Crew of the USS *Alabama*. May I have your attention, please? This is your captain. An attempted mutiny has been put down. Because of this heinous act, we shall maintain a constant security alert. Authorized movement in two-man teams only.

"In absence of further radio communications, and under direct orders from the National Command Authority, we will achieve launch depth as quickly as we can for strategic missile launch! Set condition 1SQ. Spin up missiles one through five and twenty through twenty-four for strategic launch. The use of nuclear weapons has been authorized. This is the captain. Lieutenant Zimmer is the new XO. That is all.''

Intently listening to Ramsey's announcement from the locked confines of the wardroom were Hunter and his handful of supporters. The junior members of this group were already having serious doubts, and even the COB was beginning to question his actions.

"So what do you figure, does the navy still hang mutineers?" asked the COB, from his seated perch at the forward end of the mess table.

Hunter remained standing at the table's head and responded to this comment with an argumentative fervor. "Look, this is not a mutiny! I was doing it by the book."

"It's not about the damn book!" snapped the COB. "If those rebels are gonna launch and we sit here and do nothing, who's gonna stop them? Huh? Half of me's glad the captain came back. What if he's wrong? What if he's wrong? Goddamn it! What if the captain's right?"

Hunter shared the very same concerns, but he held his ground. "No orders are valid if they're wrong."

From his position seated at the COB's right, the TSO chimed in. "The thing is, we really don't know for sure if they're wrong!"

The rest of the men grumbled in agreement. Hunter sensed their confusion and he spoke to them with a pleading urgency.

"What if Radchenko has surrendered already and it's all over? That could very well be what that partial EAM was trying to inform us of. But Ramsey's decided to ignore that possibility. As it stands now, we are going to launch our Tridents. Believe me, the Russians are gonna see them coming. In response, they're gonna send up their own birds, and after our warheads pass in the air, bingo! What we have is a full-scale nuclear war!''

Hunter's argument hit home, and as the men realized that this nightmare scenario could very well come to pass, the COB spoke for each one of them. ''So, what do we do to stop the launch, other than sit here and worry ourselves sick?''

Hunter directly returned the COB's discouraged glance and answered. ''Trust me, COB. All that I can tell you is that I've already set the wheels in motion.''

With the end of his long watch rapidly approaching, Danny Rivetti put his hand in his pocket and fingered the keys that the XO had given him. Hunter had been extremely secretive about the transfer and had merely mentioned that Danny would know what to do with the keys when the time was right.

Captain Ramsey's recent announcement to the crew indicated that Hunter's short command had ended. That could only mean that the XO and his supporters were in serious trouble.

Regardless of this fact, Danny still thought well of Hunter. He was the type of intelligent, straight-shooting officer that the navy couldn't get enough of. And for him to have risked his entire career to wrest control of the ship from the captain meant that his motives had to have substance.

From what Danny could piece together, it all concerned the missing contents of a partial EAM that was received during the first torpedo attack.

Hunter desired to reestablish contact with Command and determine the EAM's exact contents, while Ramsey wanted to ignore it and continue carrying out the launch orders from their previous EAM.

Danny never questioned his ability to support such a launch order should that fated day ever come. That was the reason for their existence. As one of his instructors so aptly put it, the *Alabama* was nothing more than the ultimate in stealthy, underwater missile silos. Sonar, tactical weapons, radio, engineering, and navigation—all of those functions had only one ultimate purpose, to support the successful release of their missiles should the president or his proxies ever order them to do so.

The passing of the Cold War fooled Danny into believing that the world was a safer place, especially from the unthinkable wrath of a thermonuclear war. The *Alabama* was only another weapons delivery system, which he hoped would never be utilized, in that complex game known as deterrence.

Had events in Russia really gotten so out of hand that the release of nuclear weapons was the only way to remedy the situation? Surely the Russian leaders knew that there would be no winners in such an exchange. The effectiveness of deterrence was its ability to make an enemy carefully rethink its decision to uncork the nuclear genie. One miscalculation, and the aggressor could be assured that a devastating response would rain from the sky, in the form of missiles such as the *Alabama*'s Tridents.

The XO had taken his stand on the assumption that sanity had prevailed and that the partial EAM contained this very news—standing them down from nuclear alert. As far as Danny was concerned, surely this assumption should be taken most seriously. Captain Ramsey's alternative remained the unthinkable. It would lead to nothing short of total destruction, and Danny felt that; at the very least, the captain should have taken the prudent route and reestablished contact with Command before launching their missiles.

"Sup," said one of his sonarmen from the broadband console, "it appears that our friends the whales are back. Bearing three-three-four, designate Sierra three-one."

Rivetti mechanically reported the new contact to the control room, his thoughts elsewhere. With his hand still fingering the XO's keys, Danny decided to follow once more his intuition, and he spoke matter-of-factly to the sailor who had just reported their latest biologic.

"Roth, take over, will you? I've got to take a whiz something fierce."

Unsure of his next move, Danny cautiously left the sonar room. They were currently under a security alert, which meant that all authorized movement throughout the ship was limited to two-man teams only. By proceeding on his own, Danny was directly violating that order. It wasn't the first time that he had broken the rules, and it was a spur-of-the-moment impulse that sent him down the stairway leading to the boat's third level.

As he slowly approached the bottom of the stairwell, he knelt down and spotted an armed sailor standing on the deck below, beside the closed door to the wardroom. This sentry was dressed in a black flak jacket and his presence there surely indicated that the XO was locked inside.

Danny's previous dealings with this particular sailor were extremely limited. His name was Wilford, and most of his work had kept him segregated in the reactor compartment. Danny certainly didn't have anything against the guy, and it was with sincere regret that he was forced to revert to the only plan that appeared to make any sense in this awkward situation.

As calmly as possible, Danny completed his transit of the stairwell. He turned toward the wardroom, and walked down the passageway like he owned the place.

"Hey!" challenged the startled sentry, putting his hand on his holstered pistol. "You know the drill, sailor. All movement is restricted to two-man teams only. So what the hell are you doing down here all alone?"

Trying his best to appear as innocent as possible, Danny reached into his pocket and pulled out the XO's keys. "I realize that we're under a security alert, babe. But you know how it is. It seems like I've been on sonar watch forever, and I just ran down here to grab some Joe. Hey, I found this key chain on the stairwell. Are they yours?"

Danny handed over the keys, but made certain to let go of them a fraction of a second before they made contact with the guard's outstretched hands. Wilford took the bait, and as he bent down to pick up the key ring, Danny clubbed him on the back of his neck with a solid right. The dazed sentry collapsed onto the floor headfirst, his forehead hitting the linoleum deck with a sickening crack. He was down for the count and much more, and Danny stooped, grabbed the keys, and turned for the wardroom door to unlock it.

"Freeze!" commanded a deep, no-nonsense voice from the aft passageway.

Danny did as ordered and, as he turned to see who it was that had caught him, he grimaced upon spotting the smirking face of Seaman Bennefield. His blond-haired bunkmate had a combat shotgun in his hands, and the black flak jacket that he wore only made the muscular Californian appear that much more intimidating.

"My, my, just what do we have here?" snickered Bennefield. "You ain't never gonna learn to mind your own business, are ya, Rivetti?"

Caught with his hands in the proverbial cookie jar, Danny could only think of a single response, and he innocently dangled the key chain in front of him.

"Chill out, Bennefield. I was only coming down here to relieve you on the captain's orders, and that's when I found Wilford here on the deck, and these keys on the floor beside him."

Not about to swallow such a wild tale, Bennefield skeptically shook his head. "Jesus, Rivetti, you really are some piece of work, you know that? Why don't I give the captain a call, and confirm your story?"

"What do you think I am, Bennefield, a Russian spy? At least take a look at these."

With this, Danny tossed his interrogator the key chain. Bennefield instinctively raised his free hand to catch it, and, as he did so, Danny rushed forward and slapped the barrel of the shotgun straight upward. His surprise attack caused the barrel of the shotgun to be pointed directly into Bennefield's throat. Danny's hand found the weapon's trigger, and he dared his shipmate to challenge him further.

"Let go of it, Bennefield, before I blow your fucking head off!"

Bennefield released the shotgun. Danny grabbed it and, while aiming its barrel squarely at Bennefield's gut, beckoned toward the wardroom.

"Okay, surfer boy. Open the door!"

Bennefield's hands were shaking as he attempted to comply with Rivetti's command. He needed to use both hands to guide the first of the keys into the lock. Even then, the tumbler failed to trigger, and Danny was suddenly fearful that they weren't the correct keys after all. His fears were alleviated seconds later when the next key in the series proved to be the master. The door was opened, and Danny prodded Bennefield inside with the shotgun pushed up against his back.

The first person that Danny spotted inside was the XO. Lieutenant Commander Hunter stood at the head of the wardroom table, a look of utter surprise covering his face. The COB quickly arose from a seated position at the opposite end of the table and readily took the shotgun from Danny and signaled Bennefield to sit down.

"I'm impressed, Mr. Rivetti," said the COB proudly.

Danny tried his best to react as nonchalantly as possible. "What did you expect, Chief? After all, I did grow up in New York City."

With no time to waste, Hunter spurred his shipmates into action. "If we're gonna have a chance to stop that launch, we'd better get moving. COB, we're going to need some duct tape to tie these guys up with.''

The COB nodded in compliance with his request. ''I've got us a roll next door in the goat locker, sir.''

''Then go to it,'' instructed Hunter, who next turned his attention to the senior sonarman. ''Mr. Rivetti, you did excellent work here, son. Now, how about rounding up a couple of your shipmates to join us? Some extra muscle would be greatly appreciated.''

14

"**Weapons, conn.** Confirm target package: SLBM zero-four-eight-niner-three-slash-four . . . for missiles one through five and twenty through twenty-four. This is the captain."

"Weapons, conn. Confirm target package: SLBM zero-four-eight-niner-three-slash-four . . . for missiles one through five and twenty through twenty-four. This is the XO."

Peter Ince spoke into his chin-mounted microphone and confirmed the target package selection after double-checking the monitor screen of the main weapons systems wraparound console. The console extended almost the entire length of the missile control center's aft bulkhead. The compartment itself adjoined the missile magazine second level, with the officers' staterooms located on this same level forward.

This was Weps' personal realm, and his men were anxiously gathered around him, their eyes glued to the giant console that Ince currently sat behind. The central portion of this console monitored the condition of each of their Trident missiles. This all-important data was displayed on twenty-four rows of rectangular digit-sized buttons. Each of the rows was marked 1–24 with a vertical line of twelve separate buttons positioned beneath each number.

At the present moment the only buttons illuminated were those belonging to missiles one through five and twenty through twenty-four. Each of these buttons glowed with a bright green light, except for the bottom four, which were lit up in red and individually labeled from top to bottom 1SQ, DENOTE, PREPARE, and AWAY.

"Weapons, conn," sounded Ramsey's voice over Weps' headphones. "What is the estimated time to 1SQ?"

Weps queried his computer to get the data that efficiently popped on the monitor screen. "Conn, weapons. Estimated time to 1SQ, five minutes and counting."

1SQ referred to the state of readiness needed to precipitate a launch. It was a compilation of a multitude of factors.

Once a condition of the 1SQ was ordered, the weapons control system would begin prepping each Trident. Their three-stage, solid-fueled propulsion systems would be activated, and a complex series of diagnostic tests run to make absolutely certain that the engines were ready for lift-off.

Of equal importance was a spinning up of the latest targeting data. In order to hit a target thousands of miles distant, the missile had to know both the coordinates of the target and the precise location of the submarine at launch.

The target coordinates were known factors and had already been entered. During 1SQ, the *Alaba-*

ma's twin MK-2, MOD 7 Ship's Inertial Navigation Systems, or SINS for short, would provide the precise point of missile release. That was made possible by a complex system of electrostatically supplied gyroscopes, accelerometers, and computers, all designed to relate the movement and speed of the sub in all directions to true north. This data was continuously fed into each missile, and subjected to an extensive diagnostic test that could take some fifteen minutes to complete.

The three launch stages that followed 1SQ usually passed in quick succession. Thus once the initial spinning-up process was completed, and the 1SQ buttons turned green, the launch itself could occur in a matter of seconds.

With no way to speed up the "prep" process, Weps could only sit back and wait for the final diagnostic to be completed. The only time that he had ever fired a Trident was over a year ago, while he was participating in a Tactical Readiness Exam (TRE) aboard the USS *Rhode Island*. The launch took place off the coast of Florida, and even though it was only a practice round, it was an awesome experience, each and every detail of which he remembered to this day.

"Weapons, conn. We have attained launch depth. One-five-zero feet, and commencing to hover," reported Ramsey over the intercom.

Weps acknowledged the update, then impatiently queried his computer and passed on the results. "Conn, weapons. I show an estimated time to 1SQ of three minutes, thirty seconds and counting."

It was the captain who relayed this information to the rest of the crew over the 1MC. Their cooperation would be essential for the successful release of all ten Tridents. And when the intercom growled, Weps supposed that an internal call was coming from one of his shipmates.

Weps pushed back his headphones and placed the nearest intercom headset to his ear. The familiar voice that greeted him caused goose bumps to form on his skin.

"Weps, it's Hunter. You gotta listen!"

Suddenly aware of the various launch technicians who were gathered around him, Weps spoke into the transmitter as discreetly as possible. "Where the hell are you?"

"Right now, that doesn't really matter," returned Hunter. "Peter, you cannot proceed with this insanity! There are other ships out there that can do this. You can't allow yourself to be influenced in this manner. You have to make up your own mind."

"But I have," Weps whispered.

"Like hell you have!" Hunter observed. "Once they're launched, they don't come back. You know the repercussions if we're wrong. We have to have communications. Right now, we are blind and crippled, and to launch at this moment would be sheer madness!"

Weps' gaze was drawn to the blinking computer screen, where the estimated time to 1SQ was rapidly approaching the three minute threshold. Having tried his best to put his doubts and fears aside, and just go on with the launch, Weps listened as his old friend continued passionately.

"Look, do not remove the firing trigger. Don't open the safe. Do you hear me, Peter? This is your prerogative. You're the only one with the combination. It's all up to you!"

It was with great reluctance that Hunter disconnected the line and looked out into the eyes of the COB. They had made this desperate call from the shelter of the officers' study, and Hunter could only listen impatiently as Ramsey's voice emanated from the 1MC.

"This is the captain. Estimated time to 1SQ is three minutes and counting. All hands, prepare for missile launch!"

COB nervously ran his hands through his crew cut, and voiced himself. "Dear God, is he gonna cooperate?"

Hunter shrugged his shoulders that he didn't know and rapidly dialed another number into the handset. "Radio, this is the XO. Vossler?"

The strained voice on the other end expressed great surprise. "Lieutenant Commander Hunter, sir, I thought the captain placed you under arrest."

"That's irrelevant at the moment, son," returned Hunter. "How are you coming with those repairs to the radio?"

"It doesn't look good, sir. Most of the primary circuits are beyond repair, and now I can't even get any juice flowing into what's left of the system."

"Vossler, I can't emphasize enough how important it is for you to get that system up. Hell, build a new one if you have to. But without that radio link with Command, the lives of hundreds of millions of innocent folks could very well be on the line!"

Disgusted, Hunter hung up the handset, and there was great worry in his face as he looked up to address the COB. "Damn it, COB! It all depends on so many variables that are out of our control."

The COB replied with compassion. "Easy does it, sir. All we can do is give it our best effort. And a little help from above certainly wouldn't hurt."

It was at that precise moment that Danny Rivetti rounded the passageway and entered the study. He had four of his shipmates in tow—tall, strapping lads, whose arrival brought the barest of smiles to Hunter's lips.

"I'd like to introduce four of the best junior sonarmen I've ever had the pleasure of workin' with," Rivetti said with a grin. "And they ain't afraid to get down and dirty, if you catch my drift."

"Gentlemen, it's good to have you all aboard," said Hunter. "Time's definitely not on our side, and I think our first stop should be at the small arms locker. Then we'll head up to control by way of the aft accessway in the second level missile compartment."

"Come on, sailors, let's move it!" added the COB, who led the way out into the passageway to get on with their perilous task.

"Captain, the ship is hovering in automatic at one-five-zero feet."

Frank Ramsey listened to the latest update from the diving officer without removing his gaze from the missile indicator panel. The display on the panel was an exact duplicate of the twenty-four rows of buttons comprising the main console in the missile control center on the deck below. The individual buttons had merely been miniaturized to allow the panel to fit inside the cramped confines of the control room.

Any moment now he anticipated that the glowing red 1SQ buttons belonging to missiles one through five and twenty through twenty-four would change to green. Only then could he continue with a task he had trained an entire lifetime to carry out—the launch of a Trident missile sortie in real wartime conditions.

With no doubts in his mind regarding the validity of his orders, Ramsey was confident that he had met all the safeguards that allowed such a drastic course of action to continue. To ensure that a missile couldn't be released either by unauthorized intent or accident, Command had instituted a strict series of checks and double-checks. The very panel he stood before was the perfect example of just such a redundant system, whose proper activation was necessary in order for a launch to take place.

The key activating the captain's missile indicator panel had been locked inside the safe in the OP-CON. With the arrival of a properly formatted EAM, that key was then removed along with the authenticator. Then after the authentication process was completed, the key was handed over to the captain, to be subsequently utilized to unlock the missile indicator panel.

Yet another safety mechanism was the individual missile keys that were locked away in Ramsey's safe. These keys would be removed by the captain after the arrival of an authenticated EAM, and were necessary to unlock the Trident's launch pressure generating system.

The final check lay under the control of Weps, whose safe held the missile firing trigger. This pistol grip–shaped trigger would be removed from his safe immediately after a condition of 1SQ was achieved. It would be plugged into the main missile console and used to activate the launch system and send the Tridents aloft.

In addition to all the safety steps, it was absolutely vital that the entire crew hear audible verification of the launch process from both the captain and his XO in order for a launch to take place. That was the final hurdle to clear, and it was a proper implication of the verification process that almost cost Ramsey his ability to carry out his current orders.

With his eyes still riveted on the indicator panel's ten glowing red 1SQ buttons, Ramsey thought about his XO's pigheaded intransigence. Hunter's mutinous efforts alone had almost negated the entire launch sequence. Hunter had ignored the fact that they had a valid launch order in hand and then had gone on to dare to question its legitimacy.

Such an act of cowardice on the XO's part was inexcusable to Ramsey, who had trained for decades for this day. Now that a valid EAM was in his hands, he certainly wasn't about to let a spineless fool like Hunter get in the way of his sworn duty.

A hostile power was fueling its nuclear-tipped missiles and threatening to launch an attack against the United States. This only went to prove that the breakup of the former Soviet Union hadn't made the world a safer place, as too many fools assumed. Without the centralized control of a strong Moscow, civil war bloodied the countryside and allowed dangerous ideologues such as Vladimir Radchenko to assume control of a government that still had tens of thousands of nuclear warheads in its arsenal. No, the end of the Cold War hadn't made the world a safer place at all, as current events unfolding outside of Vladivostok so aptly proved.

Ramsey's greatest fear was that the *Alabama*'s Tridents would arrive at their target too late. Delayed by their encounter with the Akula, and then by Hunter's mutiny, the effectiveness of their preemptive strike demanded that the Russian ICBMs were still in their silos. He shuddered to think what would happen if these ICBMs got skyward. Millions of Americans would die, and cities such as Seattle, Los Angeles, San Francisco, and San Diego would be effectively wiped off the face of the earth.

To think that all of those disasters could come to pass because of the foolish actions of a single individual like Lieutenant Commander Ron Hunter infuriated him. After taking a second look at Hunter's personnel file, Ramsey realized that the man was no warrior. Hunter was trained to act on a diet of policy seminars and think tanks. Following tough orders was what successful command was all about, and as Ramsey very well knew, any soldier who had too much time to think would most likely never fire his weapon!

At any second Ramsey's own convictions would be put to the test, as the launch system reached 1SQ and the final countdown began. The release of their Tridents wasn't something that he took delight in. On the contrary! As a result of their launch, thousands of the enemy would die, so that millions of Americans would live. That was his sworn duty, the consequences of which only he would have to live with.

Ramsey visualized the sequence of events that were about to take place aboard the *Alabama*. To permit firing, the outer hatch of each missile tube would open to the sea. Then Weps would squeeze the launch trigger, and the gas/steam generator system positioned at the bottom of Trident number one would roar alive. A small fixed rocket would ignite, directing its red-hot exhaust into the pool of cool water lying at the base of the launch tube. The resulting steam pressure would expel the missile from the tube. At the same time, on the other end of the tube, the launch tube closure would be shattered. This closure was a rigid, dome-shaped shell structure, designed to protect the missile's nose cone. It would be blown apart by a network of linear-shaped explosive charges that were mounted on the underside of the shell.

Once this was achieved, the missile was free to be expelled upward. Only after the thirty-two-and-a-half-ton, thirty-four-foot-high missile breached the sea's surface would its first-stage, solid-propellant booster motor ignite. A drag-reducing aerodynamic spike would then telescope into position from its stowed position in the nose, and the Trident would soar into the heavens.

To compensate for the sudden loss of the sixty-five-thousand-pound Trident, the vacant tube would be immediately backflooded with seawater. Seconds later, Trident number twenty-four would be launched in just such a manner, with number two to follow. That sequence would allow the *Al-*

abama to maintain its trim from bow to stern and port to starboard.

The entire process of launching all ten Tridents would take approximately ten minutes. No Trident submarine had ever "ripple-launched" so many missiles at one time before. And Ramsey realized that the moment of truth had finally arrived, as the 1SQ button to missile number one abruptly changed from red to green.

Ramsey took a quick glance at his ticking stopwatch and inhaled a deep, calming breath. He had to clear his dry throat before being able to address his new XO, who stood in front of him, beside the diving control console.

"Mr. Zimmer, the weapons system is at 1SQ!"

"Aye, sir," replied Zimmer. "The ship continues to hover in automatic, at a depth of one-five-zero feet."

Satisfied with the XO's report, Ramsey grabbed the intercom. "Weapons, conn. Mr. Ince, remove the tactical firing trigger!"

Ramsey expectantly glanced up to the overhead PA speaker in anticipation of Weps' reply. When a full ten seconds passed without hearing Ince's voice, Ramsey readdressed the intercom.

"Weapons, conn. I repeat. Unlock the tactical firing trigger, Mr. Ince!"

Again there was no response, and Ramsey disgustedly hung up the intercom handset. "For God's sake, now what?" he cursed.

"Mr. Zimmer!" he furiously shouted. "Take my place at the indicator panel. Absolutely no one is to touch this key. I am going down to missile con-

trol to find out what in the hell's going on down
there!''

Both lieutenants Dougherty and Westerguard
watched this confusing series of events unfold from
the navigation plot. Neither one of them was surprised when Ramsey directed his next outburst
their way.

"Dougherty, Westerguard, come with me! And
bring along a security detail."

With this said, Ramsey stormed out of the aft
doorway, his intention being to reach the missile
control center by way of the second level missile
compartment.

Currently crossing this very same compartment,
on their way to the control room, was Hunter's
group. It was the COB who cautiously led the way
down the linoleum-tiled passageway. The *Alabama*'s senior enlisted man was outfitted in a black
flak vest and was ever on the alert for any roving
security teams. They had already encountered a
pair of armed sentries in the forward portion of the
compartment. The COB had been fortunate enough
to spot them first, and he was able to silently direct
his comrades to take cover behind the nearest missile tube.

In such a careful, hide-and-seek manner, they
were able to cross nearly half of the missile magazine's length before the sound of distant voices
forced them to take cover once again. A large party
appeared to be approaching them from the aft
hatchway, and Hunter prudently signaled his men
to join him in the crawl space positioned immediately below the passageway. They accessed the

crawl space by way of a narrow, grated opening cut into the deck beside the base of missile tube number fourteen.

Danny Rivetti was the last member of the group to take cover there. No sooner did he duck below the grate than a trio of individuals swiftly passed overhead. One of these figures was dressed in khakis, and Danny counted off several seconds for the coast to clear, before discreetly peeking through the grate to identify the trespassers.

Though he could only see their backs, it only took a single glimpse at the red ball cap that the khaki-clad figure was wearing to instantly know his identity.

"Shit, it's the captain!" he informed his shipmates in a whisper. "I think Chop and Westerguard are with him, and they're headed forward with a bone in their teeth."

"I'll bet my pension that they're headed to missile control," said the COB.

"Whatever their destination," Hunter interjected, "the captain's presence down here means that he's temporarily relinquished control of the missile indicator panel. We can stop the launch from there, and that's where we'll make our stand. COB, I want you and Chief Hunsicker to enter the conn from the forward passageway. The rest of us will hit them from the aft accessway, with the removal of the captain's missile key our number one priority!"

15

Peter Ince really didn't know what he expected to accomplish with his flagrant act of defiance. Yet he had gone and done it all the same, and now he'd have to face the consequences.

The first of his shipmates to challenge his rash actions were the members of the missile control room launch team. They spoke up, even though Ince was the senior officer present. Only the fact that they had spent countless previous watches together kept him from physical harm. More fearful of the wrath that he knew would be arriving shortly from the control room than of his men's batons, Weps bravely bided his time until his inevitable confrontation with the *Alabama*'s captain came to pass. As it turned out, he didn't have long to wait.

Ramsey entered the missile control room in a whirlwind of rage. Chop and Westerguard flanked him, with a no-nonsense group of armed enlisted men taking up the rear.

"Mr. Ince," greeted Ramsey breathlessly, "what the hell is going on down here? Open that safe and remove the tactical firing key!"

"Sir," managed Weps, his heart madly pounding away, "it is my duty . . ."

"Duty?" Ramsey interrupted, not believing what he was hearing. "Son, don't you dare talk to me about duty. All I want you to do is to open that fucking safe!"

Ramsey took several steps forward. Less than two arm's lengths away from Ince, he halted and pulled out his pistol. Weps looked down the steel gray barrel of the formidable weapon that was pointed at his forehead and somehow summoned the courage to express himself.

"Sir, I can't open that safe."

"I'm counting to three, Peter," threatened Ramsey, while cocking back the hammer. "One . . . two . . . three."

Ince's eyes snapped shut in anticipation of his execution. Only when the feared shot didn't come to pass did he dare reopen them. Ramsey appeared to be waiting for this moment before lowering the barrel of the pistol and disengaging its hammer.

"Shit!" Ramsey cursed. "It doesn't do me any good to shoot you, Peter. You're the only one who knows the combination to the safe!"

In a move that took Ince totally by surprise, Ramsey turned and walked up to a trio of startled missile technicians. He surveyed their name tags, calmly positioned himself beside the shortest of the threesome, and put the gun to his head.

"However, Petty Officer Heiss here does not know the combination," continued Ramsey, a calculating gleam twinkling in his dark eyes. "There are millions of lives at stake here, and I will not let this cowardly travesty come down!''

With every intention of carrying out this threat, Ramsey cocked back the pistol's hammer and jammed the gun's barrel against Heiss' temple. Only then did he look back to the weapons console.

''Peter,'' he whispered, ''this is a very dumb decision on your part. One . . . two . . .''

''Stop it!'' Weps exclaimed, positive that Ramsey was going to shoot. ''Okay, already! I'll open the damn safe!''

Just in case Weps had any second thoughts, Ramsey kept the gun pointed at the missile technician's head while Ince went to work on the safe's lock. He needed two attempts to dial the proper combination, and only after the door swung open did Ramsey finally holster his pistol. Without a word spoken, he pushed Weps aside, reached into the safe, and pulled out the tactical firing trigger.

The trigger itself was connected to the console by way of a long, black coiled cord. It was a palm-sized, compact device, painted bright red, looking much like a pistol with its barrel removed.

''I need the fire control and launch technicians to man their consoles!'' Ramsey ordered.

The men responsible for these functions emerged from the stunned crowd of onlookers. As they seated themselves behind their corresponding consoles, Ramsey spoke to the technician seated to his left.

''Fire control, are you ready?''

''Aye, sir.''

Turning to his right, Ramsey added. ''Launcher, are you ready?''

''Aye, sir.''

''Then let's get on with it,'' Ramsey continued,

a definite impatient edge to his tone. "Prepare to initiate fire!"

With the push of a single button, the launcher caused the lights of the missile control console to flicker. A microsecond later, the button set immediately below 1SQ and labeled DENOTE turned from red to green.

"Denote one," reported the launch technician.

Weps felt his stomach tighten in a knot as he anticipated the next step in the launch process. All that remained was for the PREPARE button to turn green. Then the captain merely had to squeeze the firing trigger a single time to light up in green the final button in the series, a button appropriately marked AWAY.

The *Alabama*'s new XO was monitoring the entire launch process from his control room perch behind the missile indicator panel. Zimmer's pulse began to quicken soon after the DENOTE button on missile number one turned green. By the time the PREPARE button turned this same color a few seconds later, the first beads of sweat began rolling down his forehead.

"Prepare one!" he excitedly informed his shipmates over the 1MC.

With the next step being the launch itself, Zimmer was little prepared for the unwelcome newcomers who suddenly showed up in the forward passageway. The *Alabama*'s two senior chiefs were armed to the teeth, and from their serious expressions, it was apparent that they fully intended to use their weapons should they be provoked.

Before Zimmer could challenge the mutineers,

he found himself roughly pushed aside. Someone restrained his arms from behind, and he looked on with disbelief as Hunter rushed forward out of the aft accessway and smoothly yanked the key out of the missile indicator panel.

At the precise same moment that Hunter removed the key, Ramsey found himself briefly hesitating before pulling the firing trigger. Making the most of this historic moment, he raised the trigger for all to see, and firmly squeezed it.

Instead of the expected roar of the missile's steam release system, a perplexing silence prevailed. He squeezed the trigger one more time, and when the launch system again failed to activate, he looked back to the console. The indicator lights had turned from a steady green to a blinking red, and it was the senior launch technician who explained what had happened to terminate the launch.

"Sir, it appears that the captain's key has been removed from the missile indicator panel."

In an intuitive flash, Ramsey knew just who it was that removed this key. "Hunter!" he snarled, while dropping the missile trigger.

Taking only the time to resolutely click off his stopwatch, Ramsey rushed out of the missile control room. Once more, Chop and Westerguard followed him, with the thoroughly confused men comprising their security detail close behind.

It was with great relief that Hunter slung the lanyard holding the captain's missile key securely around his neck. The red light on the missle indicator panel blinked monotonously in front of him, and he watched as the COB squeezed in between the two seated helmsmen to resume his duties as diving officer. To the COB's left, Chief Hunsicker was the new chief of the watch, with the men that they replaced exiled to the navigation plot, along with Lieutenant Zimmer.

To keep order, Hunter directed the four armed enlisted men that Rivetti had recruited to stand guard in the aft portion of the compartment. Rivetti himself stood in front of the periscope pedestal, on Hunter's right. This gave the senior sonarman a clear view of the ceiling-mounted waterfall display, which showed the exact same data being projected onto the sonar room's broadband analyzer.

"Sonar contacts remain limited to our whale friends, designated Sierra three-four, on bearing zero-two-two, and Sierra three-five, a merchant passing to our south."

Hunter listened to Rivetti's update, his gaze locked on the rising numbers of the digital depth gauge. The *Alabama* had just passed one hundred feet, and was entering a portion of the ocean where a variety of new dangers threatened them.

"Nine-zero feet and continuing to ascend to periscope depth," the COB reported, having finally gotten settled at his new watch station.

One of the most dangerous of all submarine evolutions, the attainment of periscope depth demanded constant vigilance. With the protective ocean depths no longer available to shield them, the *Alabama* was now vulnerable to detection from above. Hostile surface ships, aircraft, and satellites constantly prowled the surface realm, their sensors tuned to detect the merest hint of a submarine's presence.

A risk of a much more immediate nature was the threat of an unwanted collision with a surface vessel. Even with the assistance of sonar, such vessels had a way of showing up topside when you least expected them. The reinforced bow of a passing merchant ship or supertanker could wreak havoc on the *Alabama*'s vulnerable sail, and it was up to Hunter to make certain that such a disaster didn't befall them.

As he prepared to move to the periscope pedestal, Hunter grabbed the intercom. "Radio, conn. Mr. Vossler?"

"Conn, radio. It's Vossler, sir," replied a familiar, harried voice over the PA.

"Mr. Vossler," continued Hunter, "we are rapidly approaching periscope depth, at which time we'll be raising the VLF mast. What's the status of our radio?"

"It's still down, sir. For some reason, the power grid's completely dead."

Hunter grimaced and did his best to remain patient. "Vossler, I don't like to give ultimatums, but I'm telling you, son! Whatever it takes, you've got to find a way to get some juice into that system!"

"Eight-zero feet," interrupted the COB.

Hunter hung up the intercom, and with the slim hope that Vossler's efforts would succeed, he stepped up onto the slightly elevated platform that roughly split the control room in half. He snapped down the handles of the boat's Mk 18 search scope and hit the ceiling-mounted lever that sent it toward the surface.

"Seven-nine feet," the COB reported.

"Seven-nine feet, aye," said Hunter as he snuggled his right eye against the periscope's rubberized lens coupling.

At a depth of seventy-eight feet, the scope's oblong viewing lens broke the sea's surface, and Hunter began a rapid, 360-degree scan of the surrounding waters. Only after he was positive that there were no immediate surface obstacles in sight did Hunter notice the bright blue, cloudless sky that beckoned invitingly from above. It was his first view of the outside world since last seeing it off the coast of Washington, a virtual lifetime ago.

A gentle swell slapped up against the lens, and Hunter soaked in this gorgeous view of a world whose beauty he had all but forgotten. Surely he had been in an alien place these past few weeks, a place where a horizon was determined by the next bulkhead.

"Sir, you should be able to see Sierra three-five," offered Rivetti from the fire control console. "Its bearing is one-six-four."

Hunter swung the scope in this direction, and, at first, the seas remained vacant. He double-checked the bearing and amplified the scope's lens magnification to its maximum power. That did the trick, and the distinctive profile of a large container ship popped into the eyepiece.

"I've got her," he reported. "She's a merchant all right, whose hold is most likely jam-packed with Japanese trade goods bound for Seattle."

The sighting of this ship proved that the outside world still existed. Yet to further verify this fact, Hunter spoke out crisply.

"COB, commence hovering. Raise the VLF mast."

"Commence hovering, raise the VLF mast, aye, sir," the COB repeated.

Hunter continued peering through the periscope, and he was able to watch as the radio mast broke the Pacific's surface. Relieved to find it undamaged, he was abruptly called away from the scope by a familiar gruff voice, firm with authority.

"I have the conn!"

Hunter looked up in time to see Ramsey enter the control room by way of the forward passageway. Chop, Westerguard, and a group of heavily armed enlisted men followed close on his heels. It was Chop who directed his men to take up positions alongside the forward bulkhead. As they raised the barrels of their weapons, Hunter's supporters did likewise, from their posts in the compartment's aft. A tense standoff ensued, with no one daring to move, except for Ramsey.

The *Alabama*'s captain didn't appear to be the least bit concerned for his safety as he steadily approached the periscope pedestal. The only person standing between Ramsey and the platform was Danny Rivetti. The senior sonarman couldn't help but be impressed with the captain's boldness, which he decided to put to the test by raising his pistol and aiming it squarely at Ramsey's chest.

"Halt, sir," he challenged.

"Shoot me," dared Ramsey, as he resolutely passed by Danny and reached the edge of the pedestal.

From his position beside the periscope, Hunter looked directly into Ramsey's glowering eyes. No words were needed to express the sheer rage that was so visible in the captain's unwavering stare.

Hunter intuitively sensed that the moment of truth had finally arrived. As calmly as possible, he stepped off the platform, and joined Ramsey beside the flickering lights of the missile indicator panel.

"Mr. Hunter, hand over my missile launch key," Ramsey demanded.

Hunter's only response was to protectively grab the key that hung from a lanyard draped around his neck. His simple act of defiance infuriated Ramsey, who took a step forward, balled up his left fist, and proceeded to slug Hunter, hard, on the point of his jaw.

The punch caught Hunter completely by surprise and knocked him off-balance. He struggled to keep from falling over, and a stinging pain shot up the right side of his face. Not about to give his attacker the satisfaction of outwardly displaying his hurt, Hunter squared back his shoulders and refocused his glance on the captain.

"My launch key, Mr. Hunter!" persisted Ramsey, totally frustrated by his opponent's doggedness.

Once more, Hunter's only reaction was to cover the key with his right hand, and again, Ramsey slugged him. The second punch caught Hunter squarely in the right cheek and sent him reeling into the indicator panel. Blood started to trickle from his nose, and he had to grab on to the panel to keep upright.

It was sheer determination that kept Hunter from protecting himself. With his boxing training, he could have easily taken Ramsey down. But that would achieve nothing. The only way for him to get his point across was to show his superior officer that no matter how much physical punishment he might dole out, Hunter would not relent.

Trying his best to ignore the blood that poured out of his nostrils, and the intense, throbbing pain that filled his bruised face, Hunter stood up straight, held the key, and silently dared Ramsey to hit him again. Ramsey did so, this time striking Hunter just below the right ear.

Once more, it was the missile indicator panel that kept Hunter from falling to his knees. He fought off a wave of nauseating dizziness, and somehow summoned the inner fortitude to face his opponent for a final round.

This time, however, as his hand grabbed for the key, Hunter noticed a sudden change in Ramsey's expression. It was almost as if Ramsey had just awakened from a deep trance. His pupils lost their focus, and he appeared momentarily disoriented.

Hunter watched as his attacker's eyes opened wide, and Ramsey began scanning the hushed control room, as if seeing it for the very first time. The concerned stares of the COB, Chief Hunsicker, and the others assembled there helped complete Ramsey's return to sanity. In an instant, the flame of his blind rage was extinguished.

"Conn, radio!" broke the excited voice of Russell Vossler over the intercom. "For a millisecond, primary power was restored! We're getting real close, sir."

This optimistic update served to complete Ramsey's transformation. Like the sudden dissipation of a thick fog, it dawned in Ramsey's mind how very much Hunter believed in himself. It was evident in the COB's behavior, and good many others, that they, too, believed in the unprecedented course of action that Hunter had chosen to pursue.

For the first time, Ramsey conceded to himself that they might be right after all. Since it would only take the receipt of a single radio message to confirm this fact or not, he reached for the intercom to yield humbly.

"Radio, conn. Vossler, this is the captain!"

"Conn, radio. Aye, captain. We are really close, sir."

With his eyes locked on Hunter, Ramsey continued. "Okay, Vossler, you get three minutes to fix the radio. Three minutes, and counting."

Ramsey hit his stopwatch, and took a seat on the edge of the periscope platform. Hunter remained standing beside the missile indicator panel. He used a handkerchief to stem the flow of blood that continued to trickle from his nostrils. His right cheek was already beginning to swell, and he watched as Ramsey pulled a cigar from his breast pocket, clipped its tip, and then lit it.

The beating that Hunter had been forced to endure was surely but a small price to pay for this chance to prove himself. The bruises would heal, but once launched, a Trident could never be recalled.

"Mr. Hunter," whispered Ramsey, a distant look in his eyes, "speaking of horses, have you ever seen those Lippizaner stallions?"

Hunter's first reaction to this non sequitur showed itself in the strange, quizzical look that filled his swollen eye. Ramsey picked up on his confusion and clarified himself.

"From Spain, Mr. Hunter. The Lippizaner stallions—the most highly trained horses in the world. Did you know that they're all white?"

Hunter couldn't believe what he was hearing, and he curtly answered, "Yes."

"Yes, you're aware that they're all white, or yes, I have seen them?" Ramsey asked.

"Yes, I'm aware they're all white, and yes, I have seen them!" snapped Hunter, an annoyed edge to his voice.

Taking a moment to regain his composure, Hunter added, "Actually at birth, they're all black, and it's over an extended period of time that the pigment changes to white."

"I didn't know that," said Ramsey, clearly impressed with this revelation. "They're quite amazing, you know. Some of the things those horses do defy belief, though the training program is simplicity itself. They just stick a cattle prod up their ass. Hell, you could probably even get a horse to deal cards. It's just a simple matter of voltage."

Hunter added, "And they're from Italy, sir. Trieste."

Ramsey exhaled a fragrant ribbon of smoke, and, ignoring Hunter, picked up his stopwatch. As he checked the time remaining for the repair effort, Hunter's glance was diverted to the helm, where the flash traffic alarm light began dimly blinking. Seconds later, Vossler's voice boomed from the intercom.

"Conn, radio. We're receiving flash traffic, Emergency Action Message! Recommend Alert One!"

Hunter was barely aware of the painful injuries

to his face as he watched Ramsey stand and address the crew over the 1MC.

"Alert One! Alert One!"

Ramsey hung up the handset, and coolly added to Hunter. "God help you if you're wrong."

"If I'm wrong, sir," Hunter retorted, "we're at war. And God help us all."

It was Ramsey who led the way into the radio room. Accompanying him into the OPCON was Hunter and lieutenants Zimmer, Dougherty, and Westerguard. They no longer had to resort to weapons to prove themselves, as all the proof they needed arrived in the form of the EAM that Vossler anxiously tore off the printer.

"Captain, we have a properly formatted Emergency Action Message," reported Darik Westerguard, after carefully reading the EAM. "For strategic missile launch, termination!"

"I concur, sir," agreed Chop.

Hunter fought off the urge to cry out in relief and joy. There was a cold expression set on Ramsey's face as he directed Westerguard to remove the authenticator. The double safe was opened, and the sealed authenticator packet taken out.

"Captain, request permission to authenticate?" asked Westerguard quietly.

Ramsey nodded. "Permission granted."

Westerguard's hands were steady as he ripped open the packet, pulled out the authenticator card, and held it up to the EAM.

"Delta. Delta. Sierra. Bravo. Zulu. Delta. Tango," he interpreted.

Chop double-checked his work, saying, "Delta. Delta. Sierra. Bravo. Zulu. Delta. Tango."

"Sir, message is authentic," concluded Westerguard.

"I concur, sir," Chop added.

Lieutenant Zimmer, who continued officially to hold the position of XO, carefully studied the message. "I concur," he said, while handing the EAM to the captain.

Though by now the EAM's legitimacy was a foregone conclusion, Ramsey intently read its contents and checked it against the authenticator.

"The message is authentic," he said with a heavy sigh.

A hushed quiet prevailed as Hunter was given the dispatch. His right eye was all but swollen shut now. Yet Hunter relished the moment as he slowly read the EAM himself.

ZZZRBA ...EMERGENCY ACTION MESSAGE (300)
FROM: NATIONAL MILITARY COMMAND
CENTER
TO: USS ALABAMA (SSBN 731)
SUBJECT: NUCLEAR MISSILE LAUNCH—
           SINGLE INTEGRATED OPERATIONAL
           PLAN (SIOP) TERMINATION.

1. SET DEFCON FOUR.
2. TERMINATE LAUNCH. ALL MISSILES.
3. UNCONDITIONAL SURRENDER—ALL
   RUSSIAN REBEL MILITARY FORCES. REBEL
   SUBMARINES RECALLED.
4. AUTHENTICATION: DELTA DELTA SIERRA
   BRAVO ZULU DELTA TANGO.

As Hunter digested the contents of the EAM, he suddenly felt as if a heavy weight had just been removed from his shoulders. An almost dreamlike feeling possessed him, as he looked up to face his captain.

"I concur, sir," he proudly said.

"Very well," returned Ramsey as he broke eye contact with Hunter, grabbed the EAM, and took off for the control room.

The boat's senior officers followed their captain into control. Hunter made it a point to survey the compartment, and he made a special effort to single out the individuals who had supported his efforts. Without the invaluable assistance of the COB, Chief Hunsicker, Lieutenant Linkletter, and Danny Rivetti, this incident could have very well resulted in a horrifying tragedy of the most unimaginable kind. It was thus with great satisfaction that Hunter acknowledged his beaming shipmates with a nod and listened as Ramsey addressed the entire crew over the 1MC.

"Crew of the USS *Alabama*. This is your captain. Set condition 2SQ. Terminate launch, all missiles. Lieutenant Commander Hunter has been reinstated as your Executive Officer. That is all. Carry on."

16

The frigid north wind blew in icy gusts, and Vladimir Radchenko pulled up the fur collar of his greatcoat in a vain effort to keep warm. The snow-covered trail he had been following for most of the morning led him into a familiar stand of mature birch trees, their sagging limbs weighted down in thick casings of sparkling ice. It was good to be back in this forest outside his dacha in Tiskovo, where the air was fresh with the clean scent of winter in the woods.

A lonely raven cried out nearby. Radchenko searched the swaying birch limbs for any sign of the creature, and the muted, distinctive clatter of an approaching helicopter caught his attention. This vehicle all too soon showed itself to be a Mil Mi-24 gunship, as it hovered directly over the birch forest. It was a lethal-looking aircraft, with a 12.7mm machine gun protruding from its snubby nose and a variety of rockets and missiles mounted on its stubby wings.

The roar of the helicopter's twin turboshaft engines rose to an almost-deafening pitch, and it flew directly over Vladimir. A glint of sunlight reflected off the binocular lenses of a commando visible in the open cabin. It didn't take much imagination on Radchenko's part to realize who that commando was searching for.

To assist the inevitable, he moved into a small, circular clearing and waved his arms overhead. The helicopter responded by dipping its nose, hovering directly over him to confirm his identity, and then soaring off in the direction of his dacha.

The return of blessed silence was most appreciated. As he reinitiated his hike, he contemplated the sobering fact that he was nothing but a prisoner now. The walls of his gulag surrounded him, in the form of an assortment of sophisticated electronic surveillance devices, a detachment of Spetsnaz commandos, and an assortment of military vehicles such as the helicopter gunship that had just buzzed him. His recent arrest orders confined him to this isolated outpost, with the warning that should he attempt to escape, he would be shot to death without question.

Ever thankful for the simple solace of this forest path, Radchenko made his way over a frozen brook. As he made his way up a gentle rise, his practiced glance spotted several fresh pawprints in the snow. They were the size of those of a large dog, and he wondered if they belonged to the magnificent grey wolf that he had encountered in these woods during his last visit. Excited by the thought, he followed the trail up a fairly steep hillside, where he entered a thick copse of lofty pines.

Radchenko halted there to catch his breath, and he remembered a similar pine thicket outside his railcar in far-off Art'om. Had it indeed been only seventy-two hours ago that he last walked those distant Siberian woods? It seemed to have taken place in another lifetime, and only went to show how the traumatic events of the past week had served to turn his entire world upside down.

It all started on that fated morning when his wife Anna arrived at his rail carriage for her surprise visit. Of course, the moment she innocently entered his temporary home, the surprise was on her, as she caught Vladimir in flagrante delicto with Tanya Markova.

No sooner had his wife of thirty years stormed out of the railcar with threats of divorce on her lips, than the phone call from Vladimir Sorokin arrived, informing him that the loyalist troops were on the move. Those same forces arrived on Radchenko's doorstep the very next day.

During the ensuing battle, thousands of his comrades died defending the missile base. Included in the long list of martyrs to the cause was his old friend Vladimir Sorokin, and the woman who had only recently rekindled his long-dormant passions, Tanya Markova.

Boris Arbatov showed his real colors at that time by turning traitor. His cowardly efforts allowed the attacking forces direct access to the missile field, even as those very same missiles were in the process of being fueled and readied for launch. But little were they prepared for the arrival of hundreds of T-72 main battle tanks, which took up positions directly above the still sealed missile silo caps. A launch now was impossible, and Vladimir was reluctantly forced to capitulate.

His capture and arrest sealed the fate of their

brief revolution. As the bulk of his troops surrendered, Vladimir was flown directly to Tiskovo under armed guard. And it was there he had been ever since, waiting for a trial whose verdict had already been determined.

At the very least, these last few days at Tiskovo had allowed him to make peace with himself. He had tried his best to save the Motherland and had failed, with a firing squad his only reward for trying. With the hope that history would one day clear his name, Radchenko decided to walk down to the reservoir that supplied Moscow with its water before returning home.

He left the thicket of pines and made his way past a stand of recently cut timber. It was there, beside the fallen trunk of an ancient cedar, that a crimson red splotch stained the snow. It appeared to be blood, a fact he confirmed as he walked over to the base of the felled cedar and spotted the frozen carcass of a huge grey wolf.

The unfortunate creature had its right forepaw caught in the serrated steel teeth of a trap. It appeared as if it had died while desperately trying to gnaw off this ensnared appendage.

Viewing this tragic scene caused Radchenko great grief. It seemed that everywhere he went recently, death followed.

His gloved hand removed a cigarette from the pocket of his greatcoat, and he wondered if this poor wolf was the same one that he had spotted before. Since they were territorial by nature, it most likely was, and Vladimir sullenly lit his cigarette. He inhaled a deep lungful of smoke, and a familiar, shooting pain coursed through his chest. It was because of such pains that he had been ordered to stop smoking, but his health made little difference now.

Vladimir leaned back against the fallen cedar, and with his eyes locked on the frozen, blood-speckled fur of the wolf, pondered the relevant symbolism of this tragic scene. Here was one of the most intelligent creatures of the forest, so noble and proud, that had resisted succumbing to death with its very last breath. It was in the wolf's futile effort to chew off its leg and escape that lay the very essence of the tragedy that had befallen the Motherland.

Much like this wolf, Mother Russia had also been ensnared in a trap. The snare's deadly teeth were formed not from steel, but from the poisoned values of Western society.

The end of so-called Cold War signaled the arrival of this fatal poison to their shores. In the guise of capitalist consumerism, it took the subtle, inviting form of rock music, movies, books, food, and fashion. Like a malignant cancer, these Western vices spread through the Motherland, and thousands of years of proud culture were cast aside for the sake of blue jeans and fast food.

As much as he hated to admit it, as long as those Western values prevailed, Russia was doomed to share the wolf's fate. Vladimir's futile efforts to reawaken his people had much in common with the wolf, as it desperately tried to gnaw off its own paw in its vain attempt at escaping.

The arrival of a numbing blast of wind underscored his somber conclusion. Pulling tight the collar of his greatcoat to counter this chill, Vladimir

Radchenko swore to himself that he would take this wolf's noble example and apply it to his remaining days of life, no matter how few these might be. For as long as the blood of life flowed through his veins, he would not give up his fight to revitalize his homeland, and make Mother Russia a great nation once again.

At the other end of the world, Lieutenant Commander Ron Hunter anxiously sat in the waiting room of Rear Admiral Mike Williams' office. The USS *Alabama* had only just arrived back at Bangor. Less than two hours earlier, Hunter had been supervising the vessel's berthing back at Delta pier. It was just as that complex process was concluding that a white navy van pulled up to the pier and parked immediately alongside them. Quick to exit this van and board the *Alabama* was Rear Admiral Williams' aide, who arrived with orders directing Hunter, Ramsey, Lieutenant Zimmer, and the COB to proceed to Sub Group 17's nearby, land-based headquarters with all due haste.

As Hunter was instructed to have a seat in the admiral's waiting room, the rest of his shipmates were invited into the inner office. Hunter was surprised that he was ostracized from the group, and he bided his time as best he could.

After a month at sea, he still didn't have his land legs. The floor below seemed to be gently rolling, and Hunter refused an offer of coffee, instead preferring to take this time alone to clear his mind.

The orders sending them back to Bangor were received shortly after the EAM terminating their missile launch arrived. An uneventful, five-day-long cruise homeward followed. Throughout this thirty-knot sprint, Captain Ramsey remained alone in his stateroom. He even took his meals there, and only showed himself during his customary morning walks through the ship with Bear.

In his absence, Hunter took virtual command of the *Alabama*. His fellow officers were extremely supportive, though little was outwardly discussed concerning the traumatic sequence of events that had taken place earlier in the patrol.

Hunter spent the majority of his free time in his cabin, where he carefully documented his experiences in diary form, while they were still fresh in his mind. As it turned out, it was a wise thing to have done, for the notebook in which his diary was written currently sat in his jacket pocket. Surely its contents would be of vital importance in the upcoming official inquest.

Hunter couldn't really say what the navy's official response to the incident would be. His greatest fear was that they'd look at his decision to assume command of the *Alabama* as an act of mutiny. If that was the case, a court-martial would be convened, public furor aroused, and his naval career effectively ruined.

His greatest asset was the truth. But he knew that the way others perceived the truth would be distorted, especially since the crisis was directly influenced by that complex factor known as the "fog of war." A submerged submarine, without the benefit of outside communications and under wartime footing, was a vastly different place than the stable confines of a court of inquiry. And regardless of the fact that his peers in the submarine fleet would be judging him, what could they possibly know of the great pressures that he had been facing? This was especially the case since no U.S. nuclear submarine had ever come that close to actually launching its missiles before.

No matter what the official finding might be, at the very least Hunter could derive satisfaction knowing that his actions had been right in the end. A needless war had been prevented, and countless millions of lives saved as a result. That was what really mattered, and whatever happened to his career was inconsequential.

With this optimistic thought in mind, Hunter looked up when the inner door to the admiral's office suddenly opened. Lieutenant Zimmer was the first one through the door, an expressionless look on his drawn face. The COB was the next to show himself. The *Alabama*'s senior enlisted man appeared genuinely relieved to have been excused. He looked blankly at Hunter and, without revealing the merest hint of what had just taken place inside the admiral's office, followed Zimmer into the outside hallway.

Hunter's nervousness intensified. In an effort to maintain his composure, he began a series of deep, calming breaths. It was as he used his handkerchief to blot dry the perspiration that had formed on his forehead that the admiral's aide showed himself at the inner doorway.

"Lieutenant Commander Hunter, could you step in here, please?"

The only other time that Hunter had visited this office was on the day he originally arrived in Bangor, a little less than two months earlier. That was just for a short courtesy visit, and so Hunter was somewhat familiar with the office's layout.

He found the admiral seated behind his traditional-style, walnut desk. Behind him was a massive picture window. Outside the window, a thick grove of hemlocks was clearly visible, giving the office a pastoral feeling. This was offset by the numerous plaques, awards, and framed pictures of submarines that filled the walls, as well as the admiral's cherished collection of submarine ball caps.

Seated in one of the four, straight-backed leather chairs set up in front of the desk was Captain Ramsey. Admiral Williams beckoned toward one of these chairs and politely greeted Hunter.

"Please sit down, Lieutenant Commander. This won't take long."

Hunter seated himself to Ramsey's immediate left, and the admiral quickly got down to business.

"As you might have very well presumed, Lieutenant Commander Hunter, I've been asked by COMSUBPAC to conduct an informal investigation into the events subsequent to the setting of condition 1SQ for strategic missile launch on board the USS *Alabama* on 6 November."

"Yes, sir," said Hunter, his pulse quickening.

"If this inquiry should proceed to a formal investigation and/or a court-martial," the admiral continued, "you are aware of your rights, and the possible consequences as spelled out by the uniform code of military justice, are you not?"

Hunter's stomach knotted. "Yes, sir," he muttered.

"Good," replied the admiral, continuing his strict monotone. "Now, on the basis of my investigation to this point, I believe I'm in a position to make my recommendation to COMSUBPAC.''

''Without my testimony, sir?'' Hunter retorted, his tone heavy with shocked disbelief.

The admiral sat forward and spoke to Hunter directly. ''Do you have a problem with that, Lieutenant Commander?''

Fearful that he was being railroaded, Hunter dared to express himself. ''I might, sir.''

Strangely enough, his defensive response caused a slight smile to turn the corners of the flag officer's distinguished face. ''Indeed,'' he thoughtfully remarked. ''Well, let's give this a try anyway. You ought to be able to live with this.''

Pausing briefly, the admiral sat back in his chair before continuing. ''Based upon preliminary testimony from the personnel involved in said incident aboard the *Alabama*, I find that officers and enlisted men alike conducted themselves in a manner consistent with the best traditions of the navy and the interests of the United States.

''The officers and enlisted men upheld the system, and when the occasion called for it, the system upheld the crew, though just barely. I therefore recommend that the inquiry into this incident be closed at the soonest possible date. Furthermore, based in no small part on Captain Ramsey's request and recommendation that he be allowed to retire at his earliest convenience, and that Lieutenant Commander Hunter be given his own command at the earliest opportunity. Any questions, gentlemen?''

''No, sir,'' returned Ramsey softly.

Pleasantly stunned by what he had just heard,

Hunter responded with a bit more passion. "No, sir!"

Ten minutes later, Hunter found himself leaving the headquarters building with Frank Ramsey at his side. The thick fog that had persisted in the area all morning had dissipated to reveal a cloud-speckled, blue sky. This gorgeous weather perfectly fitted Hunter's mood, and he momentarily halted at the building's exterior stairway to soak in the warm, midmorning sun. A songbird sang out nearby, and Hunter realized how very much he had missed the simple glories of nature, something that landlubbers too often took for granted.

The excited yelping of a dog drew his gaze to the nearby parade ground. An enlisted man was in the midst of a spirited game of fetch with Bear, and Hunter sighed contentedly.

"Oh, by the way, Mr. Hunter," said Ramsey as he pulled a cigar out of his pocket. "You were right, and I was wrong. Lippizaners are from Italy, not Spain."

Caught off guard by this unexpected remark, Hunter turned to face Ramsey. The veteran returned his glance with a wink and a crisp salute. Hunter returned his salute. Then, without a further word spoken, Frank Ramsey continued on to the parade ground to collect his dog, leaving Ron Hunter alone to face a promising future.

ABOUT NAVAL SUBMARINE BASE (SUBASE), BANGOR

Covering nearly 7,000 acres, SUBASE Bangor, located in Silverdale, Washington, is a pleasant balance of untouched forest land, award-winning operational and administrative facilities, attractive service and housing areas, bordered by beautiful mountain ranges and the pristine waters of Hood Canal.

SUBASE Bangor History

SUBASE Bangor's military history began in 1942 when it became the site for shipping ammunition to the Pacific theater during World War II. After the Navy purchased land near the town of Bangor for approximately $18.7 million, the U.S. Naval Magazine was established in June 1944 and began operations in January 1945.

From World War II, through the Korean and Vietnam conflicts, until January 1973, Bangor continued its role as a U.S. ammunition depot responsible for shipping conventional weapons abroad.

The Navy announced the selection of Bangor as homeport for the first squadron of TRIDENT submarines in 1973. An Environmental Impact Statement was published in July 1974 and construction began in October 1974. On 1 February 1977, SUBASE Bangor was officially activated. In May

1987, SUBASE Bangor was awarded the Commander in Chief's Installation Excellence Award or the "Best Base in the Navy" award. In June 1989, the Secretary of the Navy presented SUBASE Bangor the Environmental Quality Award for "effectively melding the operational requirements of the Navy with the national objectives of protecting and improving the environment."

Trident

TRIDENT is the Navy's third generation fleet ballistic missile program. It is part of the Nation's strategic deterrent triad which also includes land-based missile systems and manned bombers. TRIDENT, named for the three-pronged spear of mythology's King Neptune, can be broken down into three specific and equally important components: the missile, the submarine, and shore-based support.

Missile

The TRIDENT I, or C-4 missile, represents a quantum leap in technology and capability of the fleet ballistic missile (over the POLARIS/POSEIDON predecessors). The missile has a range of more than 4,000 nautical miles, over 1,500 nautical miles farther than POLARIS.

The longer range missile allows the submarine to operate in patrol areas 10 to 20 times greater than in the past. By increasing the range of the missile, the Navy has reduced its dependence on overseas bases. As soon as a TRIDENT submarine leaves port and submerges, it is on station and operational. The TRIDENT missile provides the United States with a survivable, reliable, sea-based strategic deterrent system that will be effective for many years to come.

The TRIDENT II, or D-5 missile, is deployed on TRIDENT submarines operating out of Kings Bay, Georgia. It is larger and more sophisticated with even greater capabilities.

TRIDENT I Missile Statistics

Length	34 feet
Diameter	6 feet
Range	4,000 nautical miles
Weight	71,000 pounds
Cost	Approximately $13 million each

Submarine

The TRIDENT is quieter, faster, larger and more powerful than any other submarine in the U.S. fleet. The OHIO Class submarine offers significant improvements and advantages over the POLARIS/POSEIDON programs in equipment design and it represents the most modern technology in the world. The reactor and propulsion plant are designed to operate more quietly with a 30-year life and longer periods between overhauls. The sonar features an increased detection range and improved analysis capability.

Displacing 10,500 tons more than a POLARIS and having eight more missile tubes, the TRIDENT is a significant advance over the POLARIS. Additionally, TRIDENT refits save money by using integrated modular components, and 6-foot diameter logistics hatches (25-inch POLARIS) eliminate the need to drydock or cut through the hull to remove large equipment that cannot be repaired on board.

Currently, there are eight TRIDENTs operating from SUBASE Bangor. The USS *OHIO* arrived in August 1982 to begin the TRIDENT era of strategic nuclear deterrence. Other TRIDENTs followed: USS *MICHIGAN*, USS *FLORIDA*, USS *GEORGIA*, USS *HENRY M. JACKSON*, USS *ALABAMA*, USS *ALASKA* and the USS *NEVADA*.

Submarine Statistics

Length	560 feet
Missile tubes	24
Beam	42 feet
Draft	36.5 feet
Displacement	18,700 tons
Torpedo tubes	4
Logistics hatches	3
Decks	4
Cost	Approximately $1.2 billion each

The third component of the TRIDENT system is SUBASE Bangor. Located on the Hood Canal, SUBASE Bangor is 155 nautical miles from the Pacific Ocean with access through the Straits of Juan de Fuca. A second TRIDENT base is located in Kings Bay, Georgia.

SUBASE Bangor hosts many tenant commands

that directly support the TRIDENT program. The mission of SUBASE Bangor is:

- To support the TRIDENT launched ballistic missile system,
- To maintain and operate facilities for administration and personnel support, which includes base security, berthing, messing, and recreational services,
- To provide logistic support to other facilities in the area.

Major tenant commands at SUBASE Bangor are: Commander, Submarine Group 9; Commander, Submarine Squadron 17; TRIDENT Training Facility, Bangor; TRIDENT Refit Facility, Bangor; Strategic Weapons Facility, Pacific; Naval Telecommunication Station, Puget Sound; Personnel Support Activity, Puget Sound; Personnel Support Detachment, Bangor; Construction Battalion Unit 418; Explosives Ordnance Disposal Mobile Unit Eleven Detachment, Bangor; and Marine Corps Security Force Company, Bangor.

RICHARD P. HENRICK is the best-selling author of *Ice Wolf*, *Ecowar*, and twelve other submarine-based techno-thrillers, with over three million books in print. He has many close friends in the U.S. Navy's tight-lipped submarine community, and is one of the few civilians ever privileged to go out on patrol aboard an Ohio-class Trident submarine.